Ultimate TEMPTATIONS

K.A. ROBINSON
writing as K. ANNE

BOOKS BY K.A. ROBINSON

TORN SERIES

Torn

Twisted

Tainted

Toxic: Logan's Story

Tamed

Adam: A Torn Series Novella

TIES SERIES

Shattered Ties

Twisted Ties

DECEPTION SERIES

Deception

Retribution

STANDALONES AND NOVELLAS

Breaking Alexandria

The Consequences of Sin

Taming Alec

Steam

Prologue

Darkness surrounded me. I didn't fear it. There was nothing in the darkness that I could not defeat. I was the light, and light always overpowered the darkness, the evil. One day, we would wipe all the evil from the Earth. We were almost there. We just needed the final piece to complete the puzzle.

I stared down at that piece as she slept. She was beautiful. I'd known she would be, but I hadn't thought she would be *this* beautiful. She looked like an angel as she slept peacefully in her bed. She would feel anything but peace if she knew she was being watched.

She was the key to our victory. She would end a war that had been raging on for thousands of years. There had already been so many souls lost to the darkness. For so long, it'd felt like we were fighting for nothing.

But now, I could see the light once again. She had no idea just how important she was. If she knew, she would probably try to run, but you couldn't run from fate. You couldn't fight Death. When her time here on Earth was up, I would make sure that she followed me to the gates of Heaven. There was no other option. If she fell into the hands of Hell, we would all be doomed. I couldn't let that happen. No matter what I had to do, I would make sure that she ended this once and for all.

Something caught my eye in the darkness. I looked up to see a shape emerging from the shadows, encompassing her bedroom.

My stomach sank as I stared into eyes that were identical to my own.

"Brother. What a surprise."

"What are you doing here, Cain?" I asked as I stared at my twin.

"I'm here for the girl, just like you are, Asher," Cain said as he stared at me. A hint of a smile was playing on his lips.

I glared at him. "She's ours."

He laughed quietly so that he wouldn't wake her. "You're wrong. It's her decision to make. We both know that."

"I'm here to ensure she makes the right choice."

"As am I." He paused to grin at me again. "May the best brother win."

I grinned back. I would.

One

Three months and two days—that was it. I smiled as I marked yet another day off my calendar. I could handle three more months.

It had already been six months since everything went to hell. It'd been six months since my mother lost her ever-loving mind. It'd been six months since she was forced into a mental institute. It'd been six months since I became the social leper of our hometown.

Six months ago, I had been the popular girl, the girl everyone wanted to be. All it had taken was one mental breakdown from my mother for me to become nothing more than gossip. My old friends had dropped me without a second thought. A few of them would give me pitying looks from time to time, but most of them pretended that I didn't exist. That was fine with me. I'd rather be invisible than pitied. I didn't want or need their pity.

My hometown, Shinnston, a small town in northern West Virginia, had just over two thousand people in it. Living in a town that small meant that everyone and their mother knew your business, so when my mother had gone crazy and decided that I needed to die to serve the Gods, everyone knew it. By the time I had been released from the hospital only a few hours later with a concussion and bruised ribs, I was the talk of the town.

I would've been forced into foster care if it wasn't for my uncle. Even though I was only a few months shy of eighteen, it didn't matter. My dad had run out on us before I was even born, leaving my mom to raise me in the town's one and only trailer park. If it wasn't for my uncle, we would've lost even that. More times than I could count, he'd helped my mom pay her bills after she'd spent her meager wages on alcohol.

Once she had been taken away, he'd stepped in and become my official guardian. Living together had been an adjustment for each of us, but we were both trying. Soon, I would turn eighteen and graduate. Then, he'd never have to worry about taking care of me again. You could bet your happy ass that I'd be running as far away from this town as I could without looking back. I'd had enough of this place to last me a lifetime.

My mom always had a drinking problem, something she blamed my nonexistent father for, but the six months leading up to her breakdown had been horrible. If she hadn't been at work, she had been wasted. I should've seen the signs, but I hadn't, and I'd almost paid with my life. But in my defense, who would have thought that they'd come home to a mother attacking them with a kitchen knife? I sure as hell hadn't.

I shouldered my bag and headed for my bedroom door. I glanced at the mirror hanging on the wall before I left. An average girl with bright blue eyes and light-brown hair stared back at me. I wasn't ugly by any means, but I didn't have the look that the models in the fashion magazines did, and I was okay with that. I'd much rather have a few curves anyway. The only thing I hated about myself was my nose. In my opinion, it was far too big for my face, but there wasn't much I could do about that.

Uncle Jack smiled at me when I walked into the kitchen. He was in his late thirties. We looked absolutely nothing alike, except for our hair color. He was well over six feet tall where I was lucky to hit five foot five inches. Where I was of average build, he was stick thin. His skin was pale, and his face was fixed in a permanent frown. It made me sad to realize that he hadn't started to look like that until my mother went crazy. She had tried her hardest to drag us down with her.

"Morning, Ella," he said.

I walked toward the front door. "Morning. I'm off to school. I'll see you later." I waved as I grabbed my keys, and then I headed outside.

That was our usual morning routine.

I never had my own car when I lived with my mom. Since Uncle Jack had taken me in, he'd let me use his spare car whenever I needed it. It was nice to know that I had my own transportation instead of relying on others to get me to where I needed to go—not that I had anyone else to rely on anymore, but still.

The drive to school would take me exactly six minutes. Over the last few months, I had figured out exactly how long it would take for me to get from my uncle's house to school. I always arrived just as the bell rang every day, so I wouldn't have to awkwardly stand around while everyone either stared at me or pretended I didn't exist.

Today was no different. I heard the bell ring just as I reached the front doors of my school.

I hurried inside and up the stairs to my locker. No one even noticed me as I passed by them. My ex-best friend, Jenny, walked by without even glancing in my direction. Her minions—Anna, Rose, and Megan—followed close behind her. I let myself miss my old life for a split second before mentally slapping myself. It was stupid to miss something that I never really had. If those girls really cared about me, they never would've abandoned me, and they sure as hell wouldn't have spread rumors about me and how I'd caught the crazy from my mom.

Forget them all. I didn't need them.

I shoved my bag into my locker and grabbed my binder and book for first period. I slammed my locker shut harder than I'd meant to, but no one seemed to notice my obvious aggression. I was one of the first to arrive in my history class. It was by far my favorite class. I loved learning how our ancestors had screwed up over and over, yet we'd still survived their stupidity. It was a miracle.

A group of girls walked into the room and sat down in front of me. I tried to ignore their conversation, but they made it almost impossible. From the sound of it, something major was happening.

"Oh my God! Did you see them? I think I'm in love!" a blonde, Stacey, said as she fanned herself.

"I know what you mean. And there are *two* of them. I wouldn't mind spending some alone time with both of them—at once." Stacey's friend added.

They burst out into laughter just as our teacher walked into the room. She glared at them, and they quickly quieted their giggles. I tried to listen to their whispers as Mrs. Carpenter took attendance, but it was no use. I shrugged as I opened my history book.

Oh well, it doesn't really matter anyway.

The rest of class was uneventful.

Once the bell rang and Mrs. Carpenter dismissed us, I walked back down the hall to my locker. After trading out books, I headed toward my second period class—math. Just as I was about to walk into class, the hairs on the back of my neck stood up. I stop dead and looked around the hall. I could have sworn that I'd felt someone watching me, but no one seemed to be paying any attention to me at all.

Still feeling like I was being watched, I hurried into my class and took my seat. Amanda, the one friend I did have, was already waiting for me. I wasn't sure how it had happened, but after everyone else had ditched me, I'd ended up talking with Amanda. She was as much of a social leper as I was, so we fit together nicely. No one paid any attention to us, and I liked it that way.

Amanda could be pretty if she tried. Her hair was dark brown, and she had the prettiest brown eyes I'd ever seen. Unfortunately, she normally pulled her hair back into a messy bun and wore clothes that were two sizes too big for her. Overall, she looked sloppy and

7

unkempt. It didn't bother me in the least, but it seemed to keep the other kids away from her.

"Have you heard the news?" she asked sarcastically.

I shook my head. "Nope. What's going on?"

"Apparently, we have two new students—twin brothers. I haven't seen them yet, but from what I've heard, they're hot—like, super melt-your-panties hot."

So, that was what the girls from my first period had been talking about. Nothing exciting ever happened around here, so two new students was a big deal, especially twins.

"Have you seen them yet?"

She shook her head. "Nope, and I really don't care to. If they're as hot as everyone says, I'm sure Jenny and her minions will swoop in and snatch them up before the day is over."

"You're probably right."

Amanda liked Jenny and her friends even less than I did. I wasn't sure what had happened between them to cause Amanda to hate them so much.

I really hated Jenny. We'd been best friends since middle school, yet she had been the first person to drop me when everything happened. I'd missed a week of school as I tried to cope with what my mother had done to me. When I had come back, Jenny had pretended that I didn't exist. I'd been crushed at the time. I'd lost everything at that point, and all I'd wanted was my best friend to comfort me. I should've known something was up when she wouldn't answer my calls, but I'd refused to see the truth.

The rumors had been rampant when I returned. I'd barely made it through my first day back. By lunchtime, I'd deserted all attempts to act like nothing was wrong. Instead, I'd hidden inside the first-floor restroom and bawled my eyes out.

I never cried again after that day. I refused to let Jenny or anyone else get to me. Soon, I would escape this school, this town, and I could start over fresh. I would find new friends who didn't know my history, and I would survive. I'd thrive. Then, when I came back for our ten-year reunion, I could tell them all to take a flying leap off a tall bridge. I'd show them just how strong Ella Wilkins was.

Amanda and I compared our homework to see if we had the same answers until our teacher, Mrs. Snow, walked in. She actually shuffled more than walked. The poor woman had to be pushing eighty, but she refused to retire. I had no idea why she would want to spend her golden years trapped in a high school, but whatever.

Just as she started to take attendance, a knock sounded at the door. A second later, it opened, and a boy walked in. My mouth dropped open as Amanda gave a low whistle. This had to be one of the new twins.

Sweet baby monkeys.

I pulled my eyes away from him long enough to see that he was having the same effect on every single girl in my class. We were all staring at him with our mouths hanging open. I swore, a few girls had drool dripping down their chins.

My eyes automatically went back to him.

Jesus. How is it possible for one guy to look that good?

I watched as he approached Mrs. Snow's desk, taking in every little detail about him. His hair was dark brown, almost dark enough to be considered black. It was just long enough that it fell across his forehead. It was shaggy but definitely in a good way. His eyes were the brightest emerald green I had ever seen. He wore a plain white shirt that hid nothing. The muscles in his arms and stomach were apparent through the thin material. He had muscles that no high school guy should possess. His nose was small, feminine even, but it only enhanced his looks. I mentally traced his strong jawline with my eyes. I had never seen a man quite as beautiful as he was.

And there are two of them.

He was too beautiful. While my eyes refused to look away, my mind told me that something about him wasn't right. His beauty was almost otherworldly. I pushed the thought away as I stared at him. I didn't care where he was from as long as he hung around long enough for me to ogle him.

No one said a word as he spoke quietly with Mrs. Snow.

After a moment, she smiled at him and turned her attention to the rest of the class. "Everyone, I'd like to introduce you to our new student, Asher. He just transferred here from Colorado."

Colorado? It was obvious that I'd need to move there if all the guys in Colorado looked like Asher.

"Asher, why don't you take the empty seat next to Gabriella?" Mrs. Snow pointed at me.

I winced at my full name. I hated it. No one, except for Mrs. Snow, called me Gabriella.

Asher looked up to see where he was supposed to sit. His eyes found the empty chair beside me, and then he looked directly at me. My eyes widened as he grinned like he'd just won the lottery. Without another word, he walked over to where I was sitting. I stared straight ahead, refusing to glance over at him. If I did, I knew I wouldn't be able to look away.

Mrs. Snow continued with taking attendance and then asked for our homework assignments. After we passed them up to her, she instructed us to open our books to page two hundred twenty. I nearly jumped out of my skin when I felt someone poke my arm.

I looked over to see Asher staring at me. "What?" I whispered.

"Can you share your book with me? She forgot to give me one, and I really don't want to ask for it in the middle of class. I hate to draw attention to myself."

I almost snorted. *He hates attention?* Well, he'd better get used to it because every female at our school was going to give him plenty of it.

"Uh, sure," I mumbled.

"Thanks." He smiled as he scooted his chair closer to mine.

I caught a whiff of his cologne and sighed.

Jesus, I need to get a life.

Despite how good he smelled and how good he looked, he was just a guy—a guy who would soon learn that I was an outcast, and then he'd run away from me, screaming. With that in mind, I frowned and forced myself to pay attention to Mrs. Snow.

Class dragged by. Every time Asher accidentally brushed against me, heat would rush to my cheeks. I tried to ignore him as much as possible, only speaking when he would ask something about what the teacher was saying. When the bell rang, I almost cried in relief.

As soon as Asher scooted away from me, I grabbed my things and all but ran from the room. I didn't stop running until I made it to my locker. After tossing my math book inside and grabbing my science book, I rested my forehead against the locker beside mine.

I needed to get my act together. No boy should make me that nervous. The fact that there was another guy here who looked just like him made me shudder. I hoped that I never saw the two of them together. If I did, I might melt into a puddle at the sight.

I stepped away from the lockers and made my way toward my science class. The entire way there, I couldn't help but think about how pretty Asher's eyes were.

Two

As soon as I walked into my science class, I spotted Asher. At least, I thought it was Asher since the twin in front of me was wearing a white T-shirt. He was standing in front of the classroom, talking to the teacher, Mr. Henry.

I slid past the twin and walked to my lab table. My table partner, Jerimiah, gave me a nod, and I nodded back. Jerimiah was nice, but he was a bit of a nerd. He didn't treat me like everyone else in this school though. We weren't friends, but we got along. I was actually glad that I had him as my partner. The kid had helped me ace more than one test. Science wasn't my strong point. I'd spend hours studying just to keep up my low A.

"Everyone, we have a new student. Please welcome Asher Collins," Mr. Henry called from the front of the room.

Just like in math class, every girl stared at Asher in awe. The guys in class were either glaring at Asher for the looks their girlfriends were giving him or sizing him up. He ignored all of them as he stared at me.

I looked away, suddenly uncomfortable. I had no idea why Asher felt the need to watch me like that.

"Why don't you take the seat next to Jenny?" Mr. Henry said, pointing to the table behind me.

I groaned quietly. It was bad enough that Jenny sat directly behind me. I'd walked out of this room with spitballs in my hair more than once. Now, I'd have to listen to her flirt with Asher every day.

It's for the best.

A guy like Asher Collins was so far out of my league that our leagues weren't even on the same continent. Before my life had fallen apart, maybe I would've had a chance but not now. I was on the bottom rung of the social ladder and barely hanging on. Guys like Asher were always at the top. He might be nice to me now, but that would change once he heard the rumors about my crazy mom. I needed to get over my infatuation at first sight and move on.

Three more months.

I ignored him as he walked past my lab table and sat down at the table behind me. The moment I heard his book drop onto the table, Jenny started whispering to him. I tuned her out as I watched Mr. Henry take roll. Once that was over, he instructed us to take notes as he turned on the overhead projector. The lights above us went off, throwing the room into semidarkness, so we could see the words on the projector screen. I scribbled in my notebook as Mr. Henry talked.

I could feel someone watching me. Without thinking, I looked back to see Asher's eyes directed toward me. He tipped his lips up into a small smile. Instead of smiling back, I turned back around and started taking notes again.

For the rest of class, I could feel him watching me, but I never glanced back again. I had no idea what his deal was, but he needed to stop. All his attention would do was cause trouble between Jenny and me, if she saw him watching me. She would leave me alone most of the time, and I wanted it to stay that way.

I sighed in relief when the bell rang. Mr. Henry flipped the lights back on, so we could see our things to pack up. I grabbed my book, notebook, and purse, and then I dashed out of the room. I didn't stop until I was at my locker. I quickly threw my book and notebook inside.

Then, I hurried down to the first floor. As I made my way to the cafeteria, I saw Amanda waiting for me at the end of the hallway. She gave me a small smile when I reached her. Neither of us said anything as we joined one of the lunch lines. Once we had our food, we walked to our usual table at the back of the cafeteria. No one at the surrounding tables paid us any attention as we sat down.

I set my purse on the floor by my feet and stared down at the food on my tray. "Ugh. What is this?"

Amanda wrinkled her nose. "I think it's a hamburger. I'm seriously doubting that though."

I looked down at the gray patty on my tray. "I think they're trying to kill us."

She laughed. "It wouldn't surprise me at this point. Just think, three more months, and we'll never have to eat mystery meat again."

That brought a smile to my face. I looked around the cafeteria, taking in all the graduation flyers hanging on the walls. They were just another reminder that my time here was almost up. I'd paid for my graduation cap and gown last week. I couldn't wait for them to come in.

"So, what did you do all weekend?" Amanda took a tiny bite of her mystery burger.

"I worked Friday, Saturday, and Sunday nights. I spent Saturday with my uncle, and on Sunday, I managed to finish my report for history."

I'd been working at the local movie theater for the last six months to help Uncle Jack with bills and save money. It wasn't glamorous by any means, but it was a job. Once I left Shinnston, I would need the money to help me get started.

Uncle Jack knew my plans and understood why I planned to leave. I'd expected him to try to talk me into staying, but he hadn't. Instead, he'd told me he'd help me as much as he could. I knew I'd have to take him up on the offer until I could survive on my own two feet, but I didn't want to be a mooch. So, I saved every dime I could. I had just over six hundred dollars saved at the moment. I hoped to have a thousand by the time I left.

"I wish my mom would let me get a job. I'm sick of staying home every weekend, and it'd be nice to have some cash of my own," Amanda said.

Amanda's mother was the complete opposite of mine. She was super sweet and loved Amanda to death, but she was also overprotective. That was the reason Amanda and I almost never socialized out of school. She wasn't allowed to go to friends' houses or have sleepovers. In the past six months, we'd gone out twice together. Both times, I'd taken her to the movies and then straight home. Her mom had been waiting at the front door when I dropped her off. At least she let Amanda talk on the phone.

"Just think, only a few months until you leave for college. Then, you can do. whatever you want," I said.

"Did I tell you she tried to convince me to live at home and drive to college every day? Thank God I got those scholarships, or I probably would've had to," Amanda said, shuddering at the thought.

"Why did you pick a college so close to home?" I asked.

She shrugged. "Everyone goes to West Virginia University."

"Everyone, except for me." I picked up my burger and took a bite. While it didn't make me hurl, it wasn't something I'd want to eat on a daily basis.

"Except for you. Have you decided on where you're going yet? I know you had a few schools that wanted you."

I chewed thoughtfully. Up until my mother had gone crazy, I'd planned on attending WVU. It was located in Morgantown, about forty minutes away from Shinnston. I couldn't go there now. Almost all of our classmates planned to go there after graduation. I wanted to escape my past, not go someplace where the rumors would ruin me before I even had a chance to start fresh.

"I've narrowed it down to the University of Maryland and Texas State. I'd prefer Texas, but I'm still waiting to see if I got the scholarships I applied for. If I don't get them, I'll have to go to Maryland."

"You'll get them. They'd be stupid to pass you up, Ella. You've had a solid four-point-oh since your freshman year."

"I hope so. Maryland should be far enough away, but I don't want to take any chances."

Amanda looked away, just like she did every time I mentioned the rumors surrounding me. She never openly questioned me about what had happened that night. Truthfully, I thought she didn't want to know. Since I didn't want to talk about it, our silent agreement not to mention it worked perfectly for both of us.

"So, what do you think of the new guys?" Amanda finally asked after an uncomfortable silence.

I shrugged. "I have science class with that Asher guy, too. He's cute, which means I'm staying far away from him. I have no doubt that Jenny will have her claws in him by the end of the week."

"Yeah, but maybe they'll see what a slimy skank she is and steer clear."

I snorted. "When do guys ever stay away from Jenny?"

She looked glum. "It sucks."

I opened my mouth to respond, but I stopped when the chair beside me moved. I looked over just in time to see Asher sitting down in it. My mouth dropped open in surprise. I glanced over to see Amanda looking as shocked as I was.

"Mind if I sit with you guys?" Asher asked.

"Um, sure," Amanda said before looking at me with raised eyebrows.

Silence surrounded our table as Amanda and I stared at Asher. I had no idea why he was sitting with us.

"What on earth is this?" Asher stared at his mystery burger.

No one said anything for a minute. Finally, I started giggling uncontrollably. Asher looked confused as Amanda tried to hide her grin.

"What? What did I say?" he asked.

"Nothing," I said through my giggles. "We just asked each other the same question."

"Well, whatever it is, I'm assuming it's safe to eat?" he asked with genuine concern in his voice.

"You'll live. I think," I said.

He slowly raised the burger and took a bite. He frowned before taking a bigger bite. "It doesn't taste nearly as bad as it smells."

"I take it that school food was edible in Colorado?" I asked.

"Colorado? Oh, yeah. It was much better there."

"So, why did you move to West Virginia? I can think of forty-nine other states I'd rather live in," I said.

Asher hesitated, almost like he had to think about his answer. "Well, uh—"

"Asher, there you are."

I looked up to see Asher's double sitting down beside him.

I couldn't help but stare. *Wow, there really are two of them.*

19

Looking at them side by side was indescribable. They were stunning on their own, but putting them together was almost too much. If they hadn't been wearing different clothes, I never would've been able to tell them apart.

Coherent thought left me as I willed myself to look away, but I had no such luck.

"If you want, we can pose together for a photo and make all your teenage dreams come true." Asher's twin smirked at me.

I snapped out of my stupor at his words. *Ass.*

I glanced at Asher to see that his whole body was tense. The scowl on his face was at odds with the smirk on his brother's.

"Cain, what do you want?" Asher finally asked.

"What? Can't I sit next to my brother at lunch? I thought you might've missed me since this morning," Cain said, the smirk never leaving his face.

"Why don't you go bother someone else? I'm trying to have a conversation with Ella and Amanda," Asher said.

I was surprised that he knew my name and Amanda's. Neither of us had told him our names, so he must've heard Amanda's during roll call in math and mine in both math and science. I was impressed that he'd paid that much attention. I was also surprised by his hostility toward his brother, and I wasn't sure what that was about. He'd seemed relaxed until Cain sat down with us. Maybe they had some kind of sibling rivalry.

"Why would I do that when bothering you is so much fun?" Asher's brother glanced up at me and then Amanda. "I'm Cain."

"Nice to meet you," Amanda mumbled.

I didn't bother to reply. His snarky comment about the picture had ticked me off.

"This is the part where you tell me it's an honor to meet me," Cain said, never taking his eyes off of me.

"Why would I do that?" I asked.

"Because it's an honor."

I snorted. This guy was obviously full of himself. "Sorry, I can't say that it is. You're kind of a jerk."

Cain pasted a fake hurt expression on his face. "You wound me."

"I doubt that." I turned my attention back to Asher. "Anyway, you were telling us why you moved here."

Asher opened his mouth, but Cain cut him off, "Our mom was transferred here, and since our dad isn't in the picture, we got a one-way ticket to West Virginia. Lucky us."

"You could go back to Colorado. I doubt if anyone would mind," I said.

"But then, you couldn't look at my pretty face."

I rolled my eyes. "I could still look at Asher's if you were gone. He's just as pretty, and *he* isn't annoying."

My face turned red as I realized what I'd just said. I wanted to groan out loud. I'd been so caught up in trying to annoy Cain that I didn't think out that last statement. I glanced at Asher, noticing the smile curving his lips. His smile was just as otherworldly as he was.

My eyes landed on Cain when he laughed.

"You think we're pretty? I'm flattered, really," Cain said.

"Oh, shut up," I snapped.

"I think I'm going to like you, Ella." Cain picked up his burger. After glancing down at it, he frowned. "What the hell am I eating?"

"Mystery burger," Amanda, Asher, and I said in unison.

Three

Cain's appearance at lunch had effectively ended any further conversation. I spent the last ten minutes of lunch watching Asher frown at Cain. Cain's smirk never once left his face. That seemed to irritate Asher even more. I knew a lot of siblings didn't get along, but these two were taking it to a whole new level.

By the time the lunch bell rang, I was so relieved that I nearly cried. Before I could stand, Cain rose from his chair, leaned down, and whispered something in Asher's ear. My eyes widened in shock when Asher's body actually started shaking with anger. Amanda gave me a bewildered look before standing. After mumbling a good-bye to Asher, I rose and followed her to dump my tray.

"What was that about?" Amanda asked once we were out of the cafeteria.

I shook my head. "No clue. Those two are taking sibling rivalry a little too seriously if you ask me. I know one thing. I wouldn't want to be their mother."

Amanda frowned. "Asher seems nice. I think Cain is a jerk though."

"You think?"

She bumped my arm with hers. "Asher must like you since he sat next to you."

"Doubtful. Even if he does, after Jenny's finished with him, he'll never look at me again."

"Wouldn't it be awesome if you stole him right out from under her nose? She'd go nuclear."

I grinned. "While that's a nice thought, I won't be going out with him anytime soon. He's cute and all, but I have more important things to worry about than boys."

I waved good-bye and headed upstairs to get my English book out of my locker. Once I had it in hand, I weaved through the crushing sea of bodies, heading toward the classroom. As usual, I was one of the first ones in class. I settled down in my chair and pulled my homework out of my bag. Someone sat down beside me, but I didn't bother to look up as I double-checked my homework. English was a breeze for me. I liked it so much that I planned to get my degree in teaching high school English.

"Aren't you going to speak to me?" a voice asked from beside me.

My head snapped up. I knew that voice. I stared at its owner trying to make sure I had the right twin.

Cain was wearing a dark pair of blue jeans and a black shirt. Asher was in a white T-shirt today. As long as they didn't dress alike, I'd be able to tell them apart. If they ever decided to match, I'd just wait for Cain to open his mouth. With his attitude, it'd take me two seconds to tell them apart.

"Sure. Why not? Hi, Cain," I said calmly. I wasn't about to let him get to me again. When I was frazzled, stupid sentences would leave my mouth.

"Aw, look at you, telling us apart already," he said as he grinned.

"It's not that hard. You're in black, and Asher is wearing white. It's not rocket science."

"You're a mouthy little thing, aren't you?" he asked.

"Like you aren't," I shot back.

He shrugged. "Good point."

Our teacher, Mrs. Harrison, walked in and started taking roll. When she was finished, Cain stood and headed to the front of the room. His walk told me everything I needed to know. The boy was cocky.

Asher had said he didn't like being the center of attention, but Cain obviously thrived on it. I looked around the room, noticing almost every girl had her eyes firmly glued on his jeans. I shook my head before glancing back at Cain.

Mrs. Harrison seemed surprised to see that we had a new student. As Cain spoke quietly to her, I watched her expression change from confused to blank in just a few seconds. She nodded once and stood. She walked robotically from her desk to the supply room where she kept extra books. When she returned, she handed Cain a book. Cain said something else to her before turning and returning back to his seat.

Mrs. Harrison stared straight ahead for a few seconds before shaking her head and frowning.

That was weird.

Mrs. Harrison asked us to pass our homework to the front before walking across the room to collect them. After they were on her desk, she grabbed another stack of papers and started moving through the rows, handing each one to its owner. When she reached me, she smiled, but her eyes looked strange. Normally bright, they were now dull and almost lifeless.

"Good job as usual, Miss Wilkins." She handed a paper to me.

I looked down to see my report on *Great Expectations* that I'd turned in last week. I grinned as I shoved it under my book. I'd landed another A without even trying.

Cain surprised me when he reached out and snatched my report off my desk. He glanced at the grade at the top before turning his attention to me.

"Pretty *and* smart. Not a bad combination." He handed my paper back to me.

"Um…thanks?" I said as I took the paper from him.

"I wasn't being sarcastic for once. Plus, you told me I was pretty, so I thought I'd return the favor."

I rolled my eyes. "You're a real charmer, you know that?"

"Yep," he said as he continued to stare at me.

What is with these guys?

Apparently, the brothers felt the need to stare at me to the point where I would feel uncomfortable.

I dropped my hair so that it hung like a curtain between us. Thankful that he couldn't see my face anymore, I turned my attention back to Mrs. Harrison.

A few minutes later, a note dropped onto my desk. I picked it up and opened it.

SO, WHAT DO YOU DO FOR FUN AROUND HERE?

I glanced at Cain and rolled my eyes before folding the paper back up and tossing it to him. He frowned as he opened it, and then he wrote something else. I almost groaned when he threw it back on my desk.

YOU DON'T LIKE ME MUCH, DO YOU?

I picked up my pencil and wrote down my response.

TRY, NOT AT ALL.

I didn't bother to fold it up before tossing it on his desk. He grinned as he read my reply. I kept my eyes on the board until he tossed it back onto my desk. I shot him a glare before reading it.

THAT'S TOO BAD. I WAS GOING TO LET YOU SHOW ME
AROUND TOWN.

Is he serious? His ego needed its own postal code. I picked up my pencil again.

SOMEHOW, I THINK I'LL SURVIVE. I'M TRYING TO PAY ATTENTION.
LEAVE ME ALONE.

I threw it back on his desk. I heard him chuckle. I looked over at him as he wadded up the paper and shoved it into his pocket.

He mouthed, *Your loss.*

I rolled my eyes. *Moron.*

Cain left me alone for the rest of class. Once the bell rang, I walked out of my class and went back to my locker. I had gym next, and today was my least favorite day. Every Monday, Mr. Reynolds would force us to play dodgeball. Jenny usually used this as an excuse to show just how much she hated me. More than once, I'd left gym class with a red welt on my face.

I grabbed my gym bag out of my locker.

"What do you have next?" a voice asked from beside me.

I yelped in surprise and almost dropped my bag.

I looked up at Cain. "Are you following me?"

"Pretty much." He pointed to a row of lockers farther down the hall. "Plus, my locker's over there."

"Lovely." I slammed my locker shut. "I have gym next, which I'm going to be late for if I stand here any longer. Have a wonderful day, Cain."

I turned and headed for the stairs. I groaned out loud when I realized that Cain was still following me.

"What a coincidence. So do I," he said from behind me once we reached the first floor.

I shivered as his breath tickled my ear. Cursing my body for its moment of weakness, I ignored him as I shoved through the crowd. I didn't stop walking until I reached the girls' locker room.

Amanda was already inside. I walked over to her and started stripping down. After I was dressed in my gym clothes, I shoved my bag and clothes inside a locker and locked it. With Jenny in my class, I always made sure that I never left it unlocked. All I needed was for her to steal my pants.

"What's wrong with you?" Amanda asked as we walked into the gym.

"Nothing. Why do you ask?"

She shrugged. "You look ticked."

"Cain is in my English class. He's very…irritating."

"Everyone, line up for stretches!" Mr. Reynolds shouted after blowing his whistle.

I walked to my place in the girls' line and started my stretches. Amanda stood next to me, doing the same. After a few minutes, I heard her giggle.

"What's so funny?" I leaned down and touched my toes.

"I don't know what you did to those boys, but neither one can take his eyes off of you."

"Huh?" I asked as I looked up.

Mr. Reynolds made the girls line up on one side of the gym and the boys on the other. My eyes followed the line of boys until I found Asher and Cain. They were on opposite sides of the room, but both guys had their eyes glued on me.

I growled in aggravation. "What is their problem?"

"If I didn't know better, I'd swear Cain's undressing you with his eyes. Asher isn't too far from it either."

"That's ridiculous!" I grumbled as I turned my attention back to my toes. "They don't even know me."

"Who cares? You have two super hot guys watching your every move. Embrace it."

"Like I need any more attention." And that was exactly what I would get if those two didn't leave me alone.

After we finished our stretches, Mr. Reynolds told us to split up into our dodgeball teams. I groaned as I took my place against the wall. I looked across the gym to see Jenny smirking at me. I made a mental note to keep my face covered at all times. She looked like she was in *that* kind of mood.

"You two! Each of you join a team, and get up against the wall!" Mr. Reynolds shouted.

I watched as Asher hurried over to where I was standing. Cain rolled his eyes before joining the opposite team. I made room as Asher crowded between me and the boy standing next to me.

"What are we playing?" he asked.

"Dodgeball," I said.

"What's that?" he asked.

"Seriously? You've never played dodgeball before?"

He shook his head.

"Basically, everyone attacks each other with those balls in the center of the gym. The goal is to hit as many people as you can without getting hit yourself. Once you're hit, you're out."

"Seems simple enough," he said.

I glanced at the muscles in his arms. I had no doubt that hurtling balls at innocent students would be easy for him. "Just don't hurt anyone."

He grinned when he noticed me staring at his arms. "I wouldn't."

Mr. Reynolds blew the whistle, and everyone took off at a full sprint toward the balls—that is, everyone, except for Amanda and me. We were both smart enough to stay against the wall as balls started flying.

Over half of both teams were hit within the first five minutes. After they were gone, things got harder for me. Without as many bodies to aim for, I soon became a target. I ducked and jumped out of the way as several students tossed balls at me. One hit right beside my head, and I winced. Whoever had thrown that one meant business.

I looked up just in time to dodge another ball flying right at me. It hit the wall just as hard as the other one. I glanced at the opposing team and noticed Jenny glaring at me. Of course it had been her.

She grabbed another ball and threw it. I dropped to the ground just in time.

The next few minutes passed in a blur as I dodged ball after ball. Almost all of them were from Jenny. Finally, she managed to hit me. Luckily for me, it was in the chest instead of the face. I glared at her before walking toward the bleachers to sit down with Amanda. I winced as another ball hit me in the back.

"Whoops. Sorry, Ella. I didn't realize you were already out!" Jenny shouted sweetly.

"Skank," I muttered under my breath as I sat down.

Two seconds later, I heard Jenny shriek in protest. I looked up just in time to see a ball nailing her in the chest. She frowned across the room at Asher before walking to the bleachers. Asher shot me a smile before turning his attention back to the game. I couldn't help but smile back. He'd seen what she did to me, and he'd gone after her. I was really starting to like Asher.

For the rest of the game, my attention was split between Asher and Cain. I whistled under my breath as Cain nailed another guy hard enough to knock him down. The boy didn't mess around. I counted my blessings that it was Jenny who'd hit me instead of him.

Finally, it was just Asher and Cain still standing. I looked back and forth between the brothers. They both openly glared at each other.

"This should be entertaining," Amanda said from beside me.

"My money's on Asher," I muttered.

From across the room, Asher turned and grinned at me like he'd heard what I just said.

I rolled my eyes at myself. *That's ridiculous.*

He was twenty feet away from me in a roomful of noisy seniors, and I hadn't spoken very loud.

"Quit standing there, looking at each other, and throw the balls!" Mr. Reynolds shouted at the brothers.

Cain's glare disappeared, and his trademark smirk returned. He grabbed a ball off the floor and threw it in Asher's direction. Asher jumped out of the way just in time and grabbed a ball of his own. He threw it at Cain, and I tensed as it bounced off the wall. He'd thrown it with a lot more force than necessary.

"Come on, brother. That all you got?" Cain taunted as he tossed a ball at Asher.

On and on it went.

Both boys were throwing their balls without holding back in the slightest. The class went silent as we watched the epic dodgeball battle in front of us. My mouth dropped open when Cain did a flip in midair to avoid Asher's ball. As soon as his feet touched the ground, he tossed a ball at Asher. It missed by inches and hit the wall next to the mats. I was only a few feet away, and my eyes widened in disbelief when I noticed the indent in the wall.

That's impossible.

There was no way he could have thrown the ball hard enough to dent the wall. I was pretty sure the walls were made of concrete.

Cain growled in frustration when he saw that the ball had missed. Asher smirked as he picked up two balls at once. I watched in awe as he launched both of them at Cain. Cain dodged the first one, but the second made contact. It hit his lower stomach with enough force that he flew backward several feet.

Damn. That's going to leave one heck of a bruise.

33

"Now, that's how you play dodgeball!" Mr. Reynolds shouted.

Cain stood back up. Neither brother paid any attention to the teacher. Both were locked in a glaring contest.

Finally, Asher broke it. He glanced over at me and then back at Cain. "That all you got, *brother*?"

Four

After Mr. Reynolds stopped praising Asher and Cain for their awesome attempts at killing each other, he dismissed us.

I headed back into the girls' locker room and changed. The bell rang just as I was pulling my shirt over my head. I grabbed my bag and hurried back upstairs to my locker. I threw it inside and picked up my book for the last class of the day, home economics.

I didn't relax until the final bell rang. Cain or Asher had been in almost every single class of mine, except for history and this one. I wasn't sure if I could have handled them being in here, too. I wanted to escape both of their stares for a while.

Today, we were going to bake cupcakes. I threw myself into baking with a vengeance, trying to distract myself from the twins. By the time class ended, I had a dozen cupcakes and an A for the day.

Satisfied, I walked to my locker and threw books into my bag. I had a ton of homework to do tonight, and I wasn't looking forward to any of it.

As I made my way to the stairs, I glanced over at Cain's locker. He was nowhere to be seen. Thankful, I slipped down the stairs to the first floor. I stopped to talk with Amanda for a few minutes before heading out to the parking lot. I scanned the crowd, but neither brother appeared.

I tried not to think about the brothers on the way home. I managed but just barely. It took me singing at the top of my lungs to quiet my thoughts.

Once I was home, I headed straight up to my room to start on my homework. Uncle Jack worked long hours and usually wouldn't make it home until after ten during the week. I didn't mind. I liked being alone. I'd been alone for most of my life since my mother would either be out at a bar or passed out in her room.

I spent the next few hours working on my homework. Once it was finished, I climbed off my bed and stretched. I grabbed a pair of fuzzy shorts, my underwear, a sports bra, and a tank top before going to the bathroom to take a shower. Once that was out of the way, I headed down the stairs to find something to eat.

I was a decent cook. I'd been making my own dinner since I was ten, so I was fairly skilled in the kitchen. Even though my uncle was never home for dinner, I always made extra and put it in the microwave so that he could eat it when he got home.

Tonight, I went with quick and easy. I fried two hamburgers and put some fries in the oven. After I finished my dinner, I shoved my uncle's in the microwave and walked outside. It was almost dark.

I loved this part of the day—when the light met the darkness. The sky was bright orange, making it seem like the world was on fire.

I sat down in the porch swing and stared at the sky. With nothing to occupy me, my mind went straight to the twins. I wasn't sure where my fascination with them came from. Sure, they were attractive—okay, more than attractive—but that wasn't it. Something about them nagged at the back of my mind. I couldn't put my finger on what it was though.

I knew from lunch and gym class that Asher and Cain definitely didn't like each other. They'd skipped right over sibling rivalry and gone straight to hate. I didn't understand how two people who looked exactly the same could be so different. Asher hit me as the quiet, thoughtful type while Cain came across as cocky and arrogant.

I could definitely see myself being friends with Asher, but I wasn't sure about Cain.

Who am I kidding?

They'd hear the rumors soon enough and take off running in the other direction, just like everyone else. My mother had repeatedly poisoned my life, but this time, she'd made sure that no one would ever want anything to do with me again.

Shivers ran down my spine as I thought about *that* night. It was something I tried to block most of the time. The look in her eyes was something I'd never be able to forget though. She'd been so determined to end my life, and she felt no regret over it.

"It's pretty, isn't it?" a voice asked from the steps leading up to my porch.

I screamed and jumped backward in the swing. My eyes moved to where my surprise guest stood—Asher...or maybe it was Cain. Whoever it was, he'd changed his clothes.

"You scared the crap out of me," I finally said.

He stepped up onto my porch and walked over to where I was sitting. "My bad. I thought you saw me."

"Sorry. I wasn't paying attention. I was thinking."

"About what? My awesome body?" he asked.

Yeah, it's definitely Cain.

"You're a pain in my bum, Cain. I hope you know that. Wait, what are you doing at my house?" I asked.

I shivered as he sat next to me. I was officially freaked out. Staring at me in school was one thing, but following me home was another. It was creepy and definitely stalker material.

I scooted away from him.

He chuckled. "Chill out. I'm not following you, if that's what you're thinking."

"Then, how do you know where I live?" I shot back.

"Because I just moved in next door. I walked outside and saw you sitting here, so I thought I'd say hi."

"Oh." My eyes traveled over to the neighbor's yard. Sure enough, the *For Sale* sign that had been in the yard for months was gone. "That's...convenient."

"Isn't it? So, tell me, which window is yours? It'll be easier to sneak in late at night if I know where I'm going."

I smacked his arm. "You're hilarious. Don't you have somewhere else to be?"

"Like where?"

"I don't know. Maybe in front of a mirror, admiring your reflection?" I said sarcastically.

He laughed. "You really think I'm that arrogant?"

"Why would I think anything else? I've talked with you only a few times, and it's obvious you think you're the best thing to hit Shinnston since McDonald's."

"You know what? You're the most...alive person I've met in a long time."

I raised an eyebrow. "You normally hang out with dead people?"

"That's not what I meant, but I've been caught hanging out in a cemetery after dark on more than one occasion. I just meant that you're so free with your words. You don't hold back even if it might hurt the other person."

I shrugged. "I'm not a liar, and I don't sugarcoat anything. Life is too short to worry about stuff like that."

The incident with my mother had been proof of that.

I frowned when I noticed the look on Cain's face. It was almost as if he pitied me.

"You're right. Life is too short. You should go out and experience everything, Ella. You never know when Death is coming for you."

I stared at him with my mouth hanging open in shock. What he'd said was so...not Cain.

"Who are you? And what have you done with Cain?"

He gave me a sheepish grin. "I'm still the guy you consider to be an arrogant ass, but that doesn't mean I'm not serious sometimes."

"I'd like to point out that I only called you arrogant. You called yourself an ass. That should tell you something."

He laughed again and wrapped his arm around me. I stiffened, but he didn't seem to notice.

"I think we're going to get along great, Ella. After you blew me off in class today, I thought you were going to be a saint like my brother."

"I'm not a saint," I muttered. "I just like to stay under the radar. Getting yelled at in class isn't exactly my version of staying inconspicuous."

"Why would someone as pretty as you want to hide?" Cain asked. "I don't get it."

I gently shoved him until he finally released me. "I just do."

"Oh, come on. Tell me your dirty little secret."

I sighed. "People like to start rumors about me. I'm sure you'll hear them soon enough. They tend to leave me alone if they forget about me."

"What kind of rumors?" he asked curiously.

"It doesn't matter," I mumbled.

"If you want me to beat the shit out of someone, just let me know, and I will."

I looked up, expecting to see his smirk, but it was nowhere to be seen. Instead, a deep frown was etched into his face.

"You'd really do that, wouldn't you?" I asked.

"Yeah, I would. I hate bullies."

I shook my head. "I can't figure you out, Cain. Most of the time, you're cocky and sarcastic. Then, you come over here tonight, being all protective and even nice. I'm starting to think you have a split personality. Or maybe you're secretly a sweetheart."

He grinned and leaned closer until our faces were inches apart. My breath froze in my lungs as I stared into his gorgeous green eyes.

"I can promise you this, Ella. There's nothing nice about me. If you're looking for the saint, go find Asher. If you're looking for some fun, then I'm your guy."

I pulled away from him and rolled my eyes, cursing myself for letting him get that close. "You're impossible."

He leaned back and grinned. "But you like it."

I stood and walked to my front door. "I think you should go home now."

I didn't bother to glance back until after I'd closed the door. When I glanced out of the window in the door, the swing was still swaying gently, but Cain was gone. I looked out across my yard, but he was nowhere to be seen. I had no idea how he'd moved so quietly or so fast, but it freaked me out a tiny bit. He could sneak up on me at anytime, and I'd never know it.

I climbed the stairs and crawled into my bed. I kept playing my conversation with Cain over and over in my head. Despite his attitude, I couldn't help but wonder if there was more to him than he'd let on. I'd caught a glimpse of another side of him. It was too bad he didn't show it more often.

I cursed out loud as I hurried to shove my books into my backpack. I'd overslept, and if I didn't leave in the next five seconds, I was going to be late for my first class. I grabbed a marker off of my desk and quickly crossed off another day on my calendar before rushing out of my bedroom and down the stairs. I didn't bother to stop in the kitchen to tell Uncle Jack bye. He'd left early this morning for a meeting in Huntington. If he'd been here like normal, he would've woken me up when I didn't hear my alarm.

I grabbed my keys and dashed outside to where my car was parked. I threw my bag into the passenger seat and hastily shoved my keys into the ignition. I groaned when my car refused to start. The lights on the dash came on, and the car made some kind of clicking sound, but that was it.

"Are you *kidding* me?" I shouted at no one.

I leaned against the steering wheel in defeat, knowing that I wouldn't make it to school on time. I could walk, but I'd still be late. I slowly climbed out of the car, pulling my bag behind me. There was no point in walking. Besides, curling up in my bed sounded like a much better idea.

When I reached the bottom step of my porch, I heard someone calling my name. I turned to see Cain…or Asher. I wasn't sure which.

He jogged up to me and gave me a sympathetic smile. "Car trouble?"

"Yeah, the stupid thing won't start," I grumbled.

"Come on. I'll give you a ride to school."

"Um…okay," I said, surprised by his offer. I followed him across my yard to where a silver Mustang sat. "Wow. Nice car."

"Thanks." He opened his door and climbed in.

I sat in the passenger seat, still trying to figure out which brother I was with. I finally gave up once we were almost at school. He hadn't spoken a word since we started driving, which made me think I was with Asher. But after my conversation with Cain the night before, I wasn't completely sure.

"Stupid question. Asher or Cain?" I said, feeling like a moron.

He laughed. "Asher. If Cain were driving you to school, you would've thrown yourself out of the car by now. He likes to talk."

I laughed. "I'm going to make you both wear name tags, so I can tell you apart."

"It's not hard once you get to know us. I'm the nice one. He's…Cain."

"I'm sure I'll be able to eventually. Until then, I vote for name tags," I joked.

He pulled into the student parking lot and climbed out of the car. I followed quickly behind him, afraid that the bell had already rung. Once we made it inside, I sighed in relief when I noticed kids standing around the cafeteria. My relief quickly vanished as several students turned to stare at us. Most of them were girls, and they were openly glaring at me. It was because of Asher. It had to be. Something as simple as walking into school with him had brought more attention to me than I needed.

Asher didn't seem to notice as he stopped just inside the doors. I kept my eyes cast downward and pretended that I wasn't the center of attention.

"Did you get your math homework done?" Asher asked.

I nodded without looking up. "Yeah. It was pretty easy."

"Hey, what's wrong?" he asked, finally noticing my discomfort.

"Nothing," I said quietly, still refusing to look at him.

Maybe if I pretended I wasn't with him, people would go back to ignoring me. I stepped a few feet away from him and hoped that he wouldn't notice.

"Ella, what—oh," he muttered.

I glanced up long enough to see him staring at the sea of students, finally noticing that they were all staring back at us.

The bell rang, and I darted down the hallway, trying to escape as fast as possible. I heard him call my name, but I ignored him. Once I was on the second floor and away from all the curious students, I relaxed slightly. I knew I was being a coward, but I couldn't handle being the center of so many rumors again. I was tired of everyone looking down on me.

I grabbed my notebook and history book before heading to class. I settled into my seat just as a few other students walked in. None of them paid any attention to me as they took their seats. The same group of girls who had gushed over Cain and Asher yesterday walked in and took their seats in front of me. I tried to block out their conversation, but it was impossible.

"I don't know who she is. I was on the other side of the cafeteria, but all I know is that Jenny is pissed," Stacey, the leader of their group, said.

"Why?"

"Because Jenny laid claim to the Collins brothers yesterday. It's bullshit, but no one is dumb enough to cross her, except for this girl. I know one thing. I wouldn't want to be her, whoever she is."

"It's not fair! Jenny can't have both of them at once. Why not claim one and let someone else have the other?" one of her friends whined.

"You going to tell Jenny that?" Stacey asked.

"Um, no. Definitely not. I've seen the damage she can do."

As one, the girls in the group glanced back at me.

I pretended not to notice as I tried to process what they'd said. Jenny had claimed *both* as hers. Anyone who got in her way would pay the price.

I debated on faking sick and going home as I realized that Jenny was going to do everything in her power to make sure I suffered. I almost wished that I'd stayed home today.

I knew one thing. There was no way I was riding home with Asher after school. I'd rather walk than add fuel to Jenny's fire.

By the time I made it to math class, I was in a horrible mood.

Amanda took one look at me and frowned. "I take it you heard?" she asked.

"Heard what?"

"Jenny is out for blood—your blood. What did you do?"

I sighed as I opened my book. "My car wouldn't start, so Asher drove me to school. We walked in together, and it was like we were the main attraction at the circus. Everyone was staring. I guess Jenny had called dibs on Asher and Cain, so I'm now walking around with a target on my back."

Amanda shook her head. "Someone needs to put that psycho in her place."

"Tell me about it," I grumbled.

I looked up just in time to see Asher walking into the classroom. He smiled at me, but I quickly looked away. He was pretty, but he wasn't worth being tortured for the next few months. I kept my gaze on my desk as he sat down beside me.

I didn't look or speak to him throughout the entire class. Instead, I turned so that my back was all he could see. Apparently, he took the hint, and he didn't try to start a conversation with me.

"You're being mean," Amanda whispered as we were packing up our stuff.

"I don't care. He's nice, but he's not worth the trouble. Maybe if Jenny sees that I'm staying away from him, she'll leave me alone."

"You have to stand up for yourself! Where's your backbone, Ella?"

"My mother took it with her when she went to the asylum," I spit out.

That shut her up. Amanda didn't say another word as we walked out of class.

I mumbled, "See you later," before heading to my locker.

I was dreading science class more than normal. I had no idea what Jenny would have in store for me. My only hope was that she wouldn't try anything while Asher was around. She wouldn't want to make herself look bad around the guy she wanted.

I took my time at my locker and made it to science class a few seconds before the bell rang. Unable to stop myself, I glanced at Jenny. She glared at me and then smirked. Her eyes slid to Asher, and the smirk instantly disappeared when she noticed him watching her. He glanced at me and then back to her, frowning the entire time. He obviously knew something was up. Hopefully, he'd be smart enough not to ask what was wrong.

I felt Jenny glaring two holes into my back the entire time I was in class, but she never said a word to me. Instead, she focused all her attention on Asher. When the bell rang, I stopped by the second-floor restroom just to make sure my hair was spitball-free before heading down to the cafeteria.

Amanda was waiting in our usual spot.

"Sorry about earlier," I muttered. "I'm just stressed."

She shrugged. "It's okay. I'm just tired of seeing you hide. I saw how you used to be before everything happened. You were the center of attention, and you loved it. Jenny couldn't hold a candle to you back then. I don't want her or anyone else making you feel like you have to hide."

"I *do* have to hide," I said as we got in line. "Don't you remember how bad it was after I came back? I don't want to go through that again."

She sighed. "Yeah, I remember. It's bull crap that you have to hide from them! You did nothing wrong!"

As Amanda's voice grew louder, I looked around and noticed a few students watching us.

"Amanda, please be quiet," I said.

She glanced around and then frowned. "Sorry. I just get so mad."

"Don't. I only have three more months, and then I'm out of here. I can handle it."

We paid for our lunches and then walked to our table. My entire body relaxed when I realized that neither Asher nor Cain was sitting there. I looked around the cafeteria, but I didn't see either of them.

Amanda talked about her last class as I played with the pizza on my tray. I couldn't bring myself to eat. I kept looking over my shoulder, expecting Jenny to appear and dish out whatever form of torment she had planned. My stomach dropped when I noticed Asher walking over to our table. I turned away as he sat down in the seat next to me.

He sighed. "Did I do something to make you mad, Ella?"

I shook my head. "Why would you think that?"

"Because you won't even look at me. You didn't say a word to me in class either."

I glanced up to see him watching me closely. "You didn't do anything."

That was a lie. He'd done everything just by being nice to me.

"Then, what's wrong?" When I just shook my head, he looked at Amanda. "Will *you* tell me what's going on?"

"It's stupid high school drama," Amanda said.

I shot her a glare, but she ignored me.

"Jenny, the local cheerleader and snob, called dibs on you and your brother," she added.

"I'm flattered, really," Cain said as he sat down in the chair next to Amanda.

I frowned when he smirked at me.

"You shouldn't be. She's a witch with a capital B. Anyway, I guess she saw Ella with Asher this morning, and she has declared war on Ella. They used to be best friends, but now, Jenny has made it her number one priority to make Ella miserable."

Asher shook his head. "No one is calling dibs on me. I don't even know who this girl is."

"She sits beside you in science class," I told him, unable to hide my grin over the fact that he didn't even know who she was.

"Oh…crap," Asher muttered. He picked up his pizza and practically inhaled it. "She's annoying."

I grinned. At least one other person agreed with Amanda and me.

"If she's bothering you, let me know, and I'll talk to her," Asher added once his pizza had disappeared.

I shook my head. "That'll only make it worse."

"Before I say anything, I want to ask one question. If I let this girl call dibs on me, will you get into a catfight with her over me? I wouldn't mind watching that," Cain said as he grinned at me.

I picked up my fork and threw it at him.

He laughed and ducked. The fork sailed past him and uselessly dropped to the floor.

"I'll take that as a no. Don't worry. I'm not interested in any of the girls around here." He gave me a look that could melt ice. "Well, except for one maybe."

I ignored him as I picked up my pizza and took a bite. Amanda and the brothers talked, but I paid no attention to them. I was too lost in my own thoughts. I hated this school with a passion. I hated this town almost as much. I couldn't believe the same kids I'd grown up with and been friends with since kindergarten were now the ones making fun of me. Humanity as a whole sucked.

"Hi, Cain. Hi, Asher," a voice said from beside me.

I didn't even try to hide my groan as I looked up to see Jenny standing by our table. She looked flawless as usual. Her hair was tied up on top of her head in a neat arrangement of curls that the cheerleaders liked to wear. She was dressed in light-blue skinny jeans, a white T-shirt that looked like a second skin, and a pair of flats I would kill to own.

Both Cain and Asher looked up at her, but neither said a word.

Her megawatt smile dimmed a bit, but she didn't give up. "Asher already knows me, but I don't think we've officially met, Cain. I'm Jenny," she said.

Cain glanced at me before turning his attention back to her. Again, neither of the brothers said a word. I ducked my head, so she couldn't see my smile. Asher wasn't the type to flirt, but Cain definitely was. I assumed he hit on anything that was female. The fact that he was ignoring her gave him bonus points in my book.

"So, um…anyway, I wanted to see if you two wanted to sit with me and my friends." She pointed to a table across the room.

"No, thanks. We're good with Amanda and Ella," Asher said politely.

Jenny finally glanced at me and wrinkled her nose in disdain. "You don't have to be nice because Ella is sitting here, Asher. Since you're new and all, I'll let you in on a little secret. No one cool associates with Ella. Actually, *no one* associates with Ella, even the other losers. Come hang out at my table with the popular kids. It's where you two belong."

Asher frowned. "I like Ella, and I don't plan to move anytime soon."

Jenny seemed surprised by his response. "Are you serious? Ella is a freak! Haven't you heard the rumors? I promise you, they're all true. Her mom really did go crazy and try to kill her. The only reason Ella isn't in the crazy house with her is because her uncle felt sorry for her and managed to convince the police or whoever to let her stay with him. She's certifiable."

Red-hot anger swirled inside of me. Without thinking about what I was about to do, I shoved my chair back and stood. I had every intention of showing Jenny just how crazy I was. She'd tormented me for months, and I was sick of it.

Before I had the chance to throw myself at her like I'd planned, Cain and Asher were out of their seats. They stood in front of me, blocking me from Jenny.

"Let me tell *you* something, Jenny," Cain said, venom dripping from his voice. "Ella isn't the psycho. You are. You think you're cool? You are nothing. I wouldn't spit on you if you were on fire, and I have no doubt that you will be someday."

"You're not welcome at our table. You're not welcome anywhere near Ella," Asher added, the kindness in his voice long gone.

"I suggest you and your groupies stay away from her, or you'll have to deal with us. And I can promise you, it won't be pretty. We're a little out of your league." Cain's voice was pure ice.

I peeked over Asher's shoulder. Jenny's mouth opened and closed, but no words came out. I couldn't believe that Asher and Cain were defending me—especially Cain. I wasn't even sure if he liked me.

"You'll regret this," Jenny finally managed to hiss.

"Doubtful. Now, run along," Cain said, making a shooing motion with his hands.

"You're choosing that *freak* over me?" she shouted, drawing the attention of everyone in the cafeteria.

A hush settled around the room.

"She's not a freak. You though? I'm thinking you are. If I were you, I'd let everyone know that you no longer have *dibs* on us. I'd hate to see what it would do for your social life if we both publically embarrassed you." Cain paused. "Oh, wait. We just did. Move along, little girl."

Jenny glanced around the cafeteria, finally realizing that every gaze was glued on her and the brothers. Her face turned red with anger. "Both of you have just ruined any chance of fitting in."

She turned and walked away, her head held high. Without a doubt, I knew that she'd just lost a few rungs on the social ladder. Every girl in school wanted Asher and Cain. Now that they'd publically embarrassed Jenny, she was no longer the top dog.

Asher and Cain both turned to me.

"I haven't had that much fun in forever." Cain grinned.

Asher put his hand on my shoulder. "You okay?"

I nodded, but I wasn't sure if I was. It was nice to see Cain and Asher defending me like that, but Jenny's words about my mom and me had stung. No one, not even her, had said those things right to my face before. I knew what everyone in this school thought of me, but hearing it was different.

Tears clouded my eyes as I shoved Asher's hand off of my shoulder, and I ran from the cafeteria. I pushed through the front doors of the school, not bothering to see if a teacher was nearby. I couldn't go to the rest of my classes, not after that. Everyone would be talking about what had just happened, and the rumors about my mom would start back up again.

Five

I ran until I was off of school grounds. I wished that I had my car. Since it was still at home, I would have to walk all the way back to my house. I kept my head down as traffic passed beside me, Jenny's words playing over and over in my head.

It took me fifteen minutes to finally reach the side road leading to my house. I climbed the steep hill, cursing as I went. I still had another ten minutes of walking to go. My bad mood intensified at that thought.

I tensed when I heard a motorcycle pulling up beside me. I was in the bad part of town, and anyone stopping around here probably wasn't friendly. Wary, I glanced over as the rider pulled off his helmet. I stopped dead when I saw that it was Cain. *Of course he had a motorcycle.*

He shut off the engine.

"What do you want?" I asked.

"Hop on. I'll give you a ride."

I shook my head. "I don't take rides from strangers."

"Oh, come on. I'm not a stranger. You look like that hill just kicked your ass. You'll pass out before you make it to your house."

I bit my lip as I debated. I really didn't want to walk anymore, but I'd never been on a motorcycle either. They kind of scared me.

"I don't like motorcycles," I finally said.

"Have you ever been on one?" Cain asked.

"Well, no."

"Then, hop on. I promise I won't kill you. You'll be perfectly safe with me. Nothing will happen."

"Famous last words," I muttered as I walked over to the bike and climbed on. It took two attempts, but I finally made it.

Cain handed me his helmet and then started the motorcycle back up. "Hold on tight. And by the way, we're not going home just yet."

Before I could protest, he took off. I yelped as I flew backward. At the last second, I grabbed Cain's shirt to keep from falling off. I swore I'd heard him laughing at me. Once I was settled, I wrapped my arms around his stomach and hung on for dear life. He turned and headed back down the hill.

When he turned onto Saltwell Road, I leaned forward and shouted in his ear, "Where are we going?"

He shrugged. "You'll see."

I frowned, but I didn't question him further. I didn't know Cain very well, but I didn't think he'd hurt me.

I clung to him as he sped down the winding road, dodging the massive potholes as he went. I had to admit, being on a motorcycle was exhilarating. I let my fear slip away as excitement took hold. I felt free for the first time in a long time. More than that, I felt safe with Cain in control. I wasn't sure why, but he had a calming effect on me when he wasn't annoying me.

When we reached the end of the road, he turned onto the interstate and headed north. I tried to shield myself from the wind by huddling against his back. It was warm out, but the wind felt like ice as his speed increased.

I sucked in a shocked breath when Cain rested one of his hands on my knee. The heat from his hand seeped through my jeans, warming my whole body with just his touch. He didn't move his hand until after he took one of the Fairmont exits. It was only ten minutes, but to me, it felt like an eternity.

I studied the back of his head, wondering where he planned on taking me. I noticed the tip of a tattoo peeking out of the top of his shirt. The urge to pull his shirt back and peer inside to see the rest of his tattoo was almost overwhelming, but I kept my arms wrapped around him instead. If I looked, I was sure he would make some kind of perverted joke.

I stared around as we passed through town and turned down a road that led us farther away from civilization. The ride would have been beautiful if the trees were green. Instead, they were the dull brown color of winter. While the weather was definitely getting warmer, the trees were still sleeping. We drove through a thick grove of pine trees, giving us a splash of green against all the brown.

My eyes widened in surprise as we turned onto a road marked *Valley Falls Park*. I'd never been here, but I'd heard that it was beautiful. I had no idea how Cain even knew about Valley Falls since he'd just moved to the area.

Cain slowed down as we drove through the park. After a few minutes, he pulled into a parking lot and shut off the motorcycle. I released him and pulled the helmet off of my head as he climbed off the bike.

"What are we doing here?" I asked.

He shrugged. "I found this place online and wanted to check it out. I figured you might want to get away for a while, so I brought you along."

"Oh, um…thanks." I climbed off the bike and looked around.

Despite the mostly brown color of the landscape, the scenery really was beautiful. That was one thing I'd miss when I left West Virginia. I'd always loved the trees and the hills that my state was so famous for. If I attended Texas State, there was a good chance I'd never see them again.

"Come on. I want to show you something." He started walking toward a trail.

I followed closely behind. Neither of us spoke until the parking lot disappeared from sight.

"Are you planning on taking me out here to murder me?" I asked as I tripped over a rock.

His arm shot out and caught me before I fell. I looked up to see him grinning at me.

"I'd never murder you. I might assault you, but you'd be willing."

I rolled my eyes as I pulled my arm out of his grasp. "Doubtful."

We walked for a few minutes before I heard the sound of water hitting against rocks. I knew there were small waterfalls in Valley Falls, but I'd never seen them. When we rounded the corner of the trail, my mouth dropped open. Not even a thousand yards away from us was one of them. I watched in amazement as the water cascaded over the falls and into the stream.

"Oh, wow. It's beautiful," I said.

"That's nothing. Follow me," Cain said.

I raised an eyebrow, wondering how he knew so much about a place he'd never been to, but I said nothing as he continued up the trail.

I stared at his back, studying him. The cocky walk from school was nowhere to be seen. Instead, his whole body was relaxed. It was as if being out here with nothing but nature calmed him. His black shirt was tight, showing off the muscles in his back and arms. My eyes traveled further down, and I found myself blushing. Cain was an ass most of the time, which meant I shouldn't be looking at his. I shook my head to clear it.

"Just a little farther," he called from up ahead.

I'd been so lost in thought that I didn't realize that he'd picked up his speed, and he was now farther down the trail. I started walking faster, trying to catch up with him. The trail started winding uphill, and I fought to keep up with him. I obviously needed to spend less time in my room and more time working out. Since I'd quit cheerleading, I'd stopped exercising altogether.

I struggled to breathe when we reached the top of the hill. I leaned over and rested my hands against my knees as I willed my heart to stop beating out of my chest.

"You're out of shape," Cain pointed out the obvious as he stopped in front of me.

"Thanks for noticing," I wheezed.

"I'm not being mean about it. I run and lift weights all the time. You're more than welcome to work out with me."

I held up a finger until my breathing returned to normal. Once I was standing again, I looked up at him. "Are you kidding me? If I tried to run with you, I wouldn't last five minutes."

He shrugged. "So what? I'll go slow until you build up your strength."

"You're serious about this?" I asked, still unsure as to whether he was being nice or making fun of me.

"Well, yeah. What would you do if you had to run from an axe murderer?"

"Trip the person next to me," I deadpanned.

He laughed. "Somehow, I think you're talking about me."

"Depends on whether or not you were being nice to me prior to the murderer chasing us." I finally cracked a grin.

He smirked at me before holding out his hand. "Come on. You're about to see the prettiest waterfall around. Granted, that isn't really saying much since there aren't many in West Virginia, but still."

I hesitated before putting my hand in his. He turned and led me through a group of pine trees. When we emerged, I saw what he had been talking about.

The waterfall I'd seen earlier was now directly below us. My mouth dropped open in awe as we walked over to a cluster of rocks. I shrieked in surprise when he lifted me up onto one of them. His hands lingered on my hips for a second before releasing me, and then he climbed up himself. I pretended not to notice his lingering hands as I looked around.

"It's…magical," I whispered as I stared at the waterfall.

I stepped closer to the edge of the rock and looked down. I gulped before backing up a few steps. Below us were more rocks. The drop was at least thirty feet—enough to shred me if I fell.

"It's magical and dangerous," I corrected myself.

"I won't let you fall. I promise." Cain sat down on our rock.

I slowly lowered myself and wrapped my arms around my knees. The only sound was the water crashing into the rocks below. I closed my eyes and let the noise drown out everything else around me.

My head jerked up several minutes later when Cain started talking. I had almost forgotten that he was with me.

"When I was younger, Asher and I lived next to a small waterfall. We would go out and play by it whenever we could."

"That's cool. What's it like, having a sibling? I always wanted one, but my mom told me no. I understand why now, but I didn't know how babies were made when I was little."

Cain laughed. "Well, when a super sexy guy takes a girl to a waterfall, clothes start to disappear, and then—"

"Cain," I warned.

"I just thought I'd help you out in case you were still unsure."

"Anyway," I said, unable to hide my grin, "tell me about you and Asher."

"There's not really much to tell," Cain said quietly.

"I call bull. You two can barely speak to each other without shooting death glares. Aren't twins supposed to be super close to each other or something?"

He shook his head. "It's not that simple. Asher and I have a complicated relationship. We've never been on the same side. We've spent so long being enemies that it's all I can remember about him most of the time."

"You guys are in high school. I'm sure that once you graduate and start your own lives, you'll realize how stupid you're both being."

"I doubt that. Asher and I will never see eye to eye. We chose different paths, and there's no coming back from that."

"What do you mean?" I asked, confused. "Like, you're going to different colleges when you graduate?"

He laughed. "Something like that. Asher's always been the good brother, the one who does what he's supposed to. I'm the one no one wanted. I was too rebellious. I made my own choices instead of simply doing what I was told." He shook his head. "It doesn't even matter. What's done is done."

"I still don't understand," I said softly.

"You will eventually." He glanced over at me, and his expression turned dark. "You'll wish you didn't once you know."

"You're so strange. You know that, don't you?" I asked.

He shrugged. "It's all part of my charm."

I snorted. "Sure it is."

I turned my attention back to the waterfall, wondering what had happened between Asher and Cain. It wasn't any of my business, and I shouldn't care, but I did. I really liked Asher despite the Jenny drama he'd brought into my life today. I was starting to like Cain, too. The more I talked to him, the more I realized that he wasn't what he seemed. And both of them had taken up for me today. I hadn't even bothered to thank either of them. Instead, I'd run away, just like I always did.

Amanda was right. I needed to grow a backbone and stop hiding from everyone. No matter what I did, the rumors about my mom would still be there. I couldn't hide from them. There was no point. Everyone already knew. I'd been judged over and over by people who I had thought were my friends. I had nothing to lose.

Anger flooded my body as I thought about the last six months. I'd done nothing to anyone. I'd been a victim. I hadn't deserved the torture I received. When I'd needed the support of my friends the most, they had turned their backs on me. They'd enjoyed my pain, relished in it.

I hated my mother for what she'd done to me. She was supposed to love and protect me. Instead, I'd always been the one to protect her. I'd taken care of her so many times in my short life. When she'd stumble through the door, so drunk she could barely walk, I'd been the one to get her to bed. I'd been the one to put the headache medicine and water on her nightstand. I'd loved her regardless of whether she loved me back. In return, she'd tried to hurt me in the worst possible way.

"You okay over there?" Cain asked.

I clenched my hands in anger as I nodded. "Yeah. Just thinking."

"Want to talk about it?" He scooted closer.

I shook my head. "Not really. I do want to thank you for today though. You and Asher didn't have to defend me, but you did. No one's ever done that for me before."

"That girl deserved it. It's as simple as that."

"You don't know me. You have no reason to take up for me, yet you did. That tells me a lot about you, Cain."

He shrugged. "I can be nice when I want to be."

"I've noticed. I think you're a good guy."

He shook his head. "I wouldn't go that far."

"No, you really are. I've spent the last six months hiding from everyone. I lost every friend I had. If I hadn't found Amanda, I probably would've lost my mind."

"What happened? I heard what Jenny said, but—"

"It's true—well, the part about my mom at least. Six months ago, I came home from a football game and found my mom waiting for me in our kitchen. She freaked as soon as she saw me. She started shouting how I had to die because it's what the Gods wanted. I mean, what kind of wack-job says something like that? Anyway, she pulled a knife out of the drawer and came after me. I've never been so scared in my life. I fought her off, but I ended up with a concussion and bruised ribs. The only reason I survived is because I knocked her out with one of her beer bottles."

Cain pulled me closer to him and wrapped his arm around me. I shivered at the close contact, but I didn't pull away.

"Hey, don't cry," he said quietly.

I hadn't even realized that I was crying. I quickly wiped away my tears. "Sorry. It's stupid to cry over it. Crying doesn't change anything. I just wish I knew what I had done to make her snap."

"You didn't do anything," he said firmly. "I'm sure your mom loves you."

"Right. Normal moms try to stab their daughters. I really felt the love."

"I know for a fact that your mom does love you. Something must have happened to cause her to do that." He hesitated. "Is your mom psychic?"

I glanced up at him. "Why would you ask me something like that?"

"It doesn't matter. Never mind." He looked away.

I gave him a questioning look, but I didn't say anything. My mom wasn't psychic, not that I believed actual psychics even existed. I had no idea why Cain would have said something like that. The question was just...strange.

"I know it doesn't seem like it, but everything happens for a reason. One day, you'll look back and understand why things happened the way they did," he said.

"One day, I'll look back and laugh at everyone who abandoned me. As soon as I graduate, I'm leaving West Virginia. I have so many plans for my future, and none of them involve the people who hurt me."

Cain tensed for a second. "What kind of plans?"

"I'm moving away, probably to Texas, and starting college. I want to be a teacher, silly as it sounds. I want to get married, have a bunch of kids, and just be happy. I have my entire life in front of me, and I'm going to make the most of it, starting now. Amanda was right. I shouldn't hide. I haven't been living since everything happened. From now on, I'm going to live. I'm not going to cower from people just because they think the worst of me."

"Sometimes, plans change, Ella," Cain said softly. "Sometimes, our futures aren't ours to control."

I shook my head. "No, I'm in control from now on. If you and Asher want to be my friends, I'm not going to try to stay away. I was horrible to Asher this morning, and it was all because I was scared of what Jenny would do."

"Jenny is nothing compared to what you'll have to face. You might as well prepare for it."

"You really think college will be that bad?" I asked.

He hesitated. "Not just college. Everything is going to be harder from now on."

"Being an adult stinks," I muttered.

"You have no idea."

For almost an hour, we sat together on the rock and watched the waterfall. I had no idea why I was so comfortable around Cain, but I was. It had nothing to do with the way he looked. It was just him. Sure, the fact that I had a super hot guy holding on to me was a plus, but more than that, it was just Cain himself. He was always so sure of himself. He had so much confidence that it made me feel confident, too. Maybe being friends with the brothers would help me deal with my shitty life until it was time for me to leave Shinnston.

Cain finally pulled away, and I instantly missed his touch.

"We'd better head back. It'll be dark soon, and without the sun, our ride back won't be fun," Cain said as he stood up and stretched.

I grabbed the hand he held out and pulled myself up. "Agreed. It was cold enough on the way here." *Until you put your hand on me. Then, I warm right up.*

We walked to the edge of the rock, and Cain jumped down. He turned and helped me clamber my way down. Once we were back on level ground, I followed him back down the trail. The walk back to the parking lot was much easier than the one earlier since it was now all downhill.

When we reached Cain's motorcycle, he handed me the helmet and then climbed on.

"Did you mean what you said about me running with you?" I asked before pulling the helmet over my head.

"Yeah. I run after school every day for an hour. You're welcome to join me."

"An *hour*? You can't be serious."

"I am. We'll start out slow for you though. We'll try half an hour and see how you do. Once you can handle that, we'll do more."

"I feel like I'm going to regret this idea."

"You will at first, but you'll be glad after you get used to it," he assured me.

"Fine, but if you laugh at me, I'm going to kick you—hard."

"I wouldn't dream of it." He started the motorcycle.

I clung to him the entire way home. I pretended it was because I was cold, but the truth wasn't quite that simple. Cain was definitely growing on me.

Six

Asher was waiting on my porch when we pulled up to my house. The moment Cain saw him, I felt his entire body tense up. I gave him a questioning look as I pulled his helmet off of my head and climbed off the bike. He ignored me as he took the helmet and put it on his bike.

"Thanks for the ride home," I said. "And for everything else." I started walking toward my house.

When he didn't reply, I turned to look back. Cain was nowhere to be seen. I looked around, thinking that he was playing a joke on me, but he was truly gone. I shook my head. I'd never seen someone move as fast as he did.

"Where did Cain go?" I asked Asher as I stepped up onto my porch.

"Inside our house. Why?" he said.

"Because he was at his motorcycle one minute and gone the next. I swear, that boy has wings."

Asher frowned, but he didn't comment. Instead, he changed the subject. "Where did you go today?"

I sat down on the swing next to him and stared out across my yard. "I had to get away, so I left school. Cain caught up to me and took me for a ride."

Asher raised an eyebrow. "When I got home from school, I stopped by to check on you, but no one answered. When Cain wasn't in gym class, I figured he was with you. I hope he didn't bother you too much. I know he's hard to handle."

"Not at all. Truthfully, Cain's not as bad as I thought he was. He's kind of growing on me."

Asher snorted in disbelief. "Cain's an asshole."

I frowned. "Sometimes, but he's also a really nice guy when he wants to be." I took a deep breath to calm my rising temper. "So, I assume you wanted to talk to me since you're sitting on my porch. What's up?"

"I wanted to check on you after what happened at lunch. That girl had no right to say those things about you and your mom. I'm sorry if I caused you any trouble by offering you a ride to school."

I shook my head. "If anyone should be apologizing, it's me. I was mean to you for no reason. The truth is, I haven't been myself for a long time. The things Jenny said about my mom are true. She did try to kill me. That was six months ago, and since then, I've been hiding from everyone. So many things were said about me after it happened, and I didn't want people to talk about me anymore, so I kind of disappeared. I was weak. You and Cain standing up for me made me realize that I shouldn't hide. Not everyone is going to make fun of me, and if they do, they aren't worth my time. You and Cain barely know me, yet you've been kinder to me than the kids I've known since kindergarten. So, thank you for what you did. It meant a lot."

Asher frowned. "I'm sorry about your mom and everything you've had to deal with since it happened. People can be really cruel when they want to be. I've never understood how some people can act the way they do."

"Me neither. Even when I was friends with Jenny, I never picked on anyone. I didn't see the point. I always knew Jenny had a mean streak, but she didn't really show it in front of me. When I came back after everything happened, the way she changed was like she was a completely different person. I've felt so alone these last few months."

He pulled me close and wrapped his arm around me. "Well, you're not alone now. You have me."

"And Cain and Amanda," I said as I grinned up at him.

He frowned. "I don't mean to sound like a jerk, but I really think you should avoid Cain. He's not what he seems. He's bad news."

The grin disappeared from my face. "I like Cain, Asher. I'm not sure what's going on with you guys, but I'm staying out of it. I like both of you. I'm not asking for you two to get along, but I *am* asking you both to respect my decision to be friends with each of you."

He ran his hand down his face in aggravation before sighing. "All right, I won't push the subject, but I want you to promise me that you'll be careful around him. I don't want him to convince you to do anything stupid."

"I'm not an idiot, Asher. No one, including you, can convince me to do something I don't want to do. I wish one of you would tell me why you dislike each other so much."

"Cain's always hated me, Ella. I tried for years to steer him in the right direction, but he refused to listen to me. Finally, I gave up and let him make his own choices. They've led him down a path that he can't come back from. He's not a good person anymore. One day, you'll see that for yourself and understand why I can't stand to be around him."

"Whatever happened between you two, you can still fix it. I know you can," I said.

He shook his head. "It's out of our hands now. Cain chose his path, and I chose mine." He pulled away from me and stood up. "I should probably head home. I'll see you tomorrow. I can give you a ride to school if you want."

"I'd appreciate that. My uncle won't have a chance to look at my car until this weekend to see what's wrong with it."

He nodded. "You can ride with me for as long as you want. I don't mind."

"Thanks, Asher. I'll see you tomorrow," I called after him.

He walked across our yards and disappeared inside his house. Then, I stood and walked into mine.

I headed straight for the kitchen and started on dinner. Usually, I would have had dinner finished already, but my trip with Cain had thrown me behind.

By the time I finished making barbeque ribs, Uncle Jack made it home. He dropped his suitcase off in his office before heading into the kitchen. I set the table and brought the ribs and mashed potatoes to the table as he grabbed two glasses.

"How was your day?" he asked once we were sitting.

"It was…okay. Jenny was her usual loving self at lunch."

I never hid what the other kids and their parents said about me. More than once, Uncle Jack had listened to me cry over their cruelness.

His brow creased in worry. "Do I need to call the school?"

He'd asked me that countless times, and I always told him no. I didn't want to involve the school any more than I had to. I could handle things on my own.

"No, I'm fine. Our new neighbors took up for me. It was kind of funny to watch them put Jenny in her place."

"New neighbors?" he asked.

"Yeah, they're twin brothers. They just moved here from Colorado with their mom. Didn't you notice the *For Sale* sign was gone?"

He shook his head. "I didn't. I've been swamped at work though, so I'm not surprised. Are these boys nice? Or should I worry about leaving you by yourself?"

I laughed. "I can handle Cain and Asher. Cain is a little rough around the edges, but once you wear him down, he's not so bad. Asher is super sweet. I really like both of them."

He relaxed a little. "It's good to hear that you've made two new friends. I hate that you're alone most of the time."

I shrugged. "I'm used to it. Mom left me alone a lot more than you do."

"Have you thought about what I asked you? About your mom, I mean."

I looked away. "The answer is still no. I'm not ready to see her again."

Over the past month, Uncle Jack had repeatedly asked me to go see my mother. I couldn't do it. I wasn't ready to see her again, and I wasn't sure if I would ever be. What did he think would happen? I doubted if she would welcome me with open arms. The woman hated me enough to try to end my life. There was no way that she'd greet me with a hug and kiss.

"I've talked with her doctors several times. She refuses to speak about that night, but they said she's doing really well otherwise. She hasn't had a drink since she attacked you, and it seems that sobriety has changed her for the better. I think if she saw you, it would help. She probably assumes you hate her."

"I *do* hate her, Uncle Jack. How could I not?"

"Your mother wasn't well, Ella. She wasn't thinking clearly. I know you haven't had the best life, but you can't turn your back on her when she needs you."

"I can, and I will." I pushed my plate away and stood. "I'm suddenly not very hungry. I'm going to my room."

He called my name as I hurried out of the kitchen, but I didn't stop. I didn't want to talk about my mom anymore. Even the mention of her was painful to me. The thought of seeing her again made me physically ill.

I showered and climbed into bed, cursing myself for leaving school without any of my books. I had homework in all three of the classes I'd shown up for, and I had no way of completing it. Hopefully, I could get it done in first period.

Just as I was drifting off, I heard a motorcycle starting up outside. *Cain.*

I shot out of bed and walked to my bedroom window. I caught a glimpse of him just before he disappeared down the road. I had no idea where he was going this late at night.

Cain was a mystery I was determined to solve.

Seven

The next morning, I dressed and headed downstairs. Uncle Jack was sitting in the kitchen, drinking coffee and looking through the papers spread out across the kitchen table. I grabbed a granola bar and started munching on it as I sat down across from him.

I glanced down at the papers, curious to see what he was working on. After a few seconds of staring at graphs, I gave up.

"By the way, my car won't start. It just clicks when I turn the key over."

He looked up at me. "I'll look at it this weekend. It might be the starter or the battery. Do you want me to give you a ride to school?"

I shook my head. "No, Asher is driving me."

He set his pen down and studied me. "I'm not sure how I feel about you being in a car with a boy."

I rolled my eyes at his attempt at parenting. "Trust me, Uncle Jack, you have nothing to worry about. I'm leaving in a few months. Boys are the last thing on my mind." *Kind of.* I wasn't so sure anymore. Two days with the Collins brothers, and I felt like my world had been turned upside down.

Satisfied with my answer, Uncle Jack turned his attention back to the papers in front of him. "Good. I'd hate to have to put the fear of God in a horny teenager."

I laughed as I stood up. "Now, that's something I'd like to see. You're too nice to be mean."

I kissed him on the cheek before heading outside.

I didn't see Asher or his car anywhere, so I walked across our yards and up the steps to their front door.

I always loved this house, but I'd never been inside. The woman who had owned it before was mean. As horrible as it was to say, I had been glad when her daughter forced the old lady to move in with her. Since she'd moved almost four months ago, I hadn't had to deal with the woman giving me the evil eye from her living room window every time I stepped outside.

The three-story house was huge compared to the other houses on this street. It even made Uncle Jack's two-story house look like a child's plaything. The layout worked so that the house was U-shaped. Just before my mean neighbor had moved, she'd paid someone to paint the exterior bright white color, and the fairly new shingles on the roof were black.

I knocked on the door and stepped back to wait for Cain, Asher, or their mom to answer. I examined the porch as I waited, noticing the potted plants hanging every few feet. A couple of pieces of porch furniture sat near a grill that my uncle would kill for.

The door swung open, and I turned back around. My mouth dropped open in surprise as I stared at a shirtless Cain…or Asher. I wasn't sure whom I was staring at, and I really didn't care. My eyes traveled down his body, taking in the hard muscles of his chest and stomach before following the deep V that disappeared into a pair of jeans that were almost low enough to be indecent. I blushed when I realized that I'd been staring for a solid minute without saying anything. My eyes quickly traveled back up his body to his face.

"Um...hi," I finally managed to say.

He grinned, the amusement in his eyes letting me know that I'd been caught staring at him. "Morning. I'm almost ready. You can come inside for a few if you want."

Asher.

If it were Cain, he would have mercilessly tortured me.

I sighed in relief before nodding. "Thanks."

He stepped aside, so I could walk into the house. I stared, taking in every little detail. I'd wanted to see the inside of this house forever.

"You can wait here or in the living room. It's on the right. I'll be back in just a minute."

I watched as Asher turned and headed up the stairs. My eyes locked on the tattoo on his back. That surprised me. Asher didn't seem like the type of person to get a tattoo. I couldn't see it well, but what I could see was impressive. The tattoo covered his entire back. I could make out the form of an angel's silhouette surrounded by heavenly light and other angels. It looked like the angel was holding a sword, but I wasn't sure.

Asher disappeared once he was at the top of the stairs, leaving me to wonder what the tattoo meant. With the angel tattooed across his back, it seemed pretty obvious that Asher was religious. Religion wasn't something I really thought about. My mother had always been too drunk to attend church on Sunday mornings. It shocked me to realize that I had no idea if she was religious or not. Since she never mentioned it, I assumed that she wasn't. As for my beliefs, I really didn't have any. If some higher being were out there, he or she had obviously forgotten about me a long time ago.

I remembered seeing the tip of a tattoo sticking out of Cain's shirt yesterday. I couldn't help but wonder if his matched Asher's. If so, the brothers obviously had something in common.

Asher returned a few minutes later. I was in the living room by that time, sitting on the couch and taking in the room. It was nice but sparsely decorated with no pictures hanging on the walls. It looked more like a display home living room rather than an actual living room. Besides the couch, chair, end tables, and television, the room was completely empty.

"Ready?" Asher asked.

I nodded and followed him outside. We walked side by side to his garage. The door lifted, and Asher's car came into view. I'd expected Cain's motorcycle to be inside, too, but it was noticeably absent.

"Did Cain leave already?" I asked.

Asher nodded. "He's usually gone by the time I wake up."

"Where does he go? Somehow, I doubt he's at school already."

"Don't know. Don't care. I'm sure he's getting in trouble wherever he is," Asher said.

We climbed into his car. I frowned but said nothing as he backed out of the garage. I hated how Cain and Asher acted toward each other. Asher was always so nice, except for when I mentioned Cain. I had expected him to at least be civil with his brother. That obviously wasn't the case.

"Did you understand the math homework last night?" Asher asked.

"I didn't bring my book home with me, so I didn't even get a chance to look at it."

"You can copy mine if you want. I think I got most of them right. Same for our science homework."

"Thanks," I said sincerely. "I wasn't really thinking when I took off yesterday."

He shrugged. "It's no big deal."

When we arrived at school, I suddenly felt nervous. I had no idea if Jenny would try anything today. Hopefully, her little showdown with Cain and Asher would keep her from her usual antics. I squared my shoulders as I climbed out of Asher's car. I wouldn't let her intimidate me any longer. She'd made me miserable for the last six months. That was far too long. From now on, I would hold my head high, and I'd stop hiding in the shadows.

"You okay?" Asher asked as we walked toward the school.

"Yeah. Why?"

"I just thought after yesterday…" He trailed off.

"I'm fine. I told you last night. I'm done hiding. From now on, I'm going to stand up for myself."

He smiled. "Glad to hear it."

I linked my arm through his just as we reached the school. Once we walked inside, I led him to a table and sat down. Since we were here a few minutes earlier than normal, I wanted to check over his homework and copy it. It wasn't my proudest moment, but it was better than getting an F on two assignments.

People turned to look at us, but no one said anything. I ignored them as Asher pulled his notebook and books out of his bag and handed them to me. We went over each problem together, double-checking to see if he had them right. Quite a few of his math problems were wrong. I showed him his mistakes and helped correct them, and then I wrote out my problems.

"I thought I was helping you, but I think it's the other way around," Asher joked.

I frowned. "Not at all. I really appreciate you doing this with me. I'm really good at math. If you want, I can help you out if you're having trouble."

He looked relieved. "Math is something I don't understand. I'll take any help I can get."

I patted his shoulder before closing his math book and opening his science book. "It's way easier than science."

"I'm good at science. We can work together to survive our classes."

"Cool." I copied his science homework without even checking it.

"Want to meet tonight? I have some stuff to do after school, but I can come by your place around eight."

"That's fine. I think I'm going to start working out with Cain. That'll give me plenty of time to exercise and then shower. I'd hate to force you to sit next to me if I smelled bad."

He grinned. "I'd sit by you even if you did stink."

"Gee, thanks," I said as I nudged his shoulder with mine.

My morning was passing by without incident. I joked around with Asher and Amanda in math class. A few of my classmates looked back at me in shock when they realized I was actually speaking, but no one said anything. In science, Jenny wouldn't even look at Asher or me. Instead, she kept her head low and stared at her book the entire time. It might've made me a bad person, but I couldn't help but grin at her sullen mood. The tables had finally turned on her. She was the one hiding, and I was the one laughing. It was Karma at its finest.

Asher, Amanda, and I stood in line to get our lunches. When we reached our table, Cain was already waiting for us. He smiled at me when I sat down next to him. His smile disappeared when Asher sat down on my other side. I frowned at both of them.

"So, how was Jenny?" Amanda asked, breaking the uncomfortable silence.

I grinned. "It was epic, Amanda. I'm not even kidding. She wouldn't even look at me. I've never seen her so...not herself."

I wrapped my arms around the brothers and hugged them. "And it's all because of these two."

Asher gave me a small smile, but Cain rolled his eyes.

"Don't get too excited. Jenny might be licking her wounds now, but she'll start acting like a bitch soon enough," Amanda said.

"Then, I'm going to enjoy this while I can." I picked up my hot dog and bit into it. "And when she comes back for me, I'll be ready. I'm done letting her push me around."

In English class, Cain sat next to me again. Other than asking if I still planned to run with him after school, we didn't say much. As we were leaving class, he informed me that I would be riding home with him. He didn't leave any room for argument from me. I bit back a sarcastic reply over being told what to do. From the smirk on his face though, he must have known what I was thinking.

I was dreading gym class. After the showdown between Cain and Asher on Monday, I was worried that they might actually attack each other. Luck was with me though as they were both assigned to the same baseball team. Unless I counted the evil glares they were shooting to each other every few minutes, gym class was passing by without incident.

"Have you figured out what's up between those two?" Amanda asked as we watched Cain walking up to home plate.

He raised the bat.

I shook my head. "Nope, and I asked them. They each just gave me a vague answer and changed the subject."

"I bet it's over a girl," Amanda said.

"Why do you say that?" I asked, my eyes never leaving Cain.

"Because guys don't fight, like, ever. If it's this bad, I can guarantee that it is over a girl. I bet you'll make it worse."

"Why do you think that? I want them to stop fighting, and they both know it!" I said as the pitcher threw the ball.

Cain hit it with enough force that the ball sailed over the fence on the opposite side of the field. He walked lazily around the field with a grin on his face.

"Show-off," I muttered as I watched him.

His gaze found mine. As he passed by the dugout, he winked at me. I rolled my eyes, knowing that he was showing off just because everyone was giving him their undivided attention.

"Because neither of them can take their eyes off of you."

"I have no idea what you're talking about," I lied.

I had noticed the brothers watching me whenever I was around them. I tried not to think about it too hard. I liked both of them, and even though they were both hot enough to make girls want to rip their clothes off, I didn't want anything more with either brother. I only had three months left here, and then I'd be leaving for college. I doubted if I'd ever see either of them again.

"Then, you're blind, Ella," Amanda said.

"It doesn't matter anyway. I'll be out of this town soon enough, and they'll be nothing more than a distant memory."

"Is that how you feel about me, too?" Amanda asked, her voice full of hurt.

I cursed myself for hurting her feelings. "No, Amanda. You know that we'll keep in touch. You're the only friend I've had these past few months. I wouldn't just walk away from you and never look back."

"Somehow, I think you'll feel the same when you leave Cain and Asher behind, too," Amanda muttered, still looking upset.

I looked up to see Asher watching me. "Doubtful."

But even I knew that I was lying.

Eight

Cain was waiting at my locker at the end of the day. I noticed him before he noticed me. I stopped and watched him. Why, I wasn't sure.

He had his back against my locker as he stared in the opposite direction of where I was standing. His shaggy hair fell into his eyes, begging for me to push it back. His expression and body language screamed, *Stay away*. Everyone seemed to take the hint and avoided walking near him.

I'd never realized just how intimidating Cain could be. I couldn't help but wonder why he even talked to me.

I forced myself to continue walking down the hall. As soon as his gaze found me, he smiled. The iciness in his gaze was replaced with such warmth that I took a step back without even realizing what I was doing.

He pushed himself off my locker and walked the few feet to where I was standing. "You ready?"

"Um, yeah. Just let me grab my books," I mumbled as I sidestepped him and went to my locker.

I refused to look at him as I stashed my book and grabbed the ones I needed. I had no clue what to think about the warmth in his eyes as he'd watched me. Cain had been nice to me more than once, but he'd never looked at me like that.

I threw my books in my backpack and turned back toward him, willing myself to calm down. Before I could say anything, he took my bag out of my hands and threw it over his shoulder.

"Come on." He walked to the staircase.

I followed behind, wondering why he was being so nice to me.

When we reached the parking lot, I saw his motorcycle parked near Asher's car.

"Wait, I need to find Asher and let him know that I don't need a ride home," I said as I looked around for Cain's twin.

"He already knows," Cain said without looking back at me.

I raised an eyebrow in disbelief. "What? You two talked? Willingly?"

He shrugged as we reached his motorcycle. "He knows. Now, get on."

He tossed me the helmet before shoving my bag into the storage compartment. I watched as he climbed onto the bike.

"You need a helmet, too, you know," I said as I pulled it over my head.

"No, I don't. I'll be fine. I'm not fragile like you." He glanced back and grinned, letting me know he was teasing.

"Your skull is as fragile as mine. Actually, I take that back. You don't need a helmet. You're too hardheaded as it is."

I climbed onto the bike and wrapped my arms around him. I pretended not to notice the hard contours of his stomach, but I failed miserably.

He started the bike and took off. I relaxed my body against his as he drove back to our houses. Just like the day before, I loved riding on his bike. Shinnston was congested with school traffic, but I still felt free.

When traffic came to a halt, he swerved off the main road and drove on the sidewalk, and I laughed. A few people shouted at us as we passed by, but I paid little attention to any of them. I should've been worried about getting in trouble, but I wasn't. I trusted Cain when I was around him. The rules didn't seem so black-and-white like I'd always thought. No, there was much more gray than I'd ever expected.

He swerved back onto the road and turned up the big hill leading to our houses. Once we reached the top of the hill, traffic pretty much disappeared.

As soon as we pulled up in front of his house, I climbed off the bike and stretched. I handed his helmet back to him, and then he grabbed my bag and tossed it to me. I shouldered it and stared at him, waiting for further instructions.

When he did nothing more than look at me, I sighed. "Are we going to run or not?"

"Yeah, but I want to change first. Jeans aren't the easiest to run in. Meet me back out here in ten." He climbed off the bike and started walking to his house.

I watched him disappear inside before walking to my own. I unlocked the door and hurried upstairs to my room.

After dropping my bag on the bed, I grabbed a pair of shorts and a tank top out of my dresser. I pulled my shirt over my head and tossed it into the hamper. Just as I was about to pull my tank top on, I caught movement outside of my window. I jerked my tank top over my head and then hurried over to my window. The only thing I saw was my yard and a darkened window in Cain and Asher's house. I stared at Cain's window, wondering if he had just watched me change clothes. After a minute, I finally gave up. There was no one at the window. As usual, I was paranoid. Still feeling uneasy, I lowered the blinds before pulling off my jeans. I shimmied into my shorts and pulled on my tennis shoes.

As I walked downstairs, I realized that the afternoon with Cain would probably end in embarrassment. I knew I was out of shape, and Cain…definitely wasn't.

When I walked outside, I didn't see Cain waiting for me, so I headed across our yards to his front door. I knocked and stepped back, waiting. After a minute, I frowned.

"Where is he?" I whispered.

"Right here."

I jumped when I felt his warm breath tickling the back of my neck. I spun to see him standing only inches away. He didn't try to hide his interest as his eyes skimmed down my body. I felt myself blushing as he stared at my legs. I suddenly wished I had worn sweatpants.

His gaze finally worked its way back up my body to my face. The warmth that I noticed in his eyes earlier was back. I wanted to take a step back again, but I held my ground. I was being stupid. Cain was attractive, but he'd never once made me nervous.

"Tell me what to do," I said. I wanted to slap myself for saying that. I knew he was going to say something perverted as he smirked.

"You can go—"

I held up my hand. "I mean, about running."

He continued to smirk at me for a minute before speaking, "We need to stretch first."

"Like in gym class?"

He nodded.

"Okay, I can do that."

We walked out into the yard. He dropped down onto the grass and started stretching his legs. I did the same, making sure to copy his every move. He seemed to notice and grinned as he stood up, and I followed right behind him. He leaned down and touched his toes for a few seconds before standing back up.

"Keep doing that. I need to run inside and grab water bottles," he said as he backed away.

I nodded and kept stretching. Without him beside me, I suddenly felt like an idiot. I continued to stretch, touching my toes, for another minute or so before finally standing up straight. I turned toward the house to see if he was coming, and I noticed him standing on his porch.

"What are you doing up there?" I asked.

"Admiring the view." He grinned like the devil.

"The view?" I asked, confused.

"Yeah, the view. Sadly, it turned around."

It took me a minute to figure out what he'd meant. When I did, I felt my face turning red in embarrassment. "You were staring at my ass?"

He jumped up onto the porch banister and then down onto the lawn. It happened so fast that I blinked twice to make sure I was seeing clearly. Before I could register his entirely too fast movements, he was standing next to me, holding out a water bottle.

"Wha—how did you do that?" I stuttered.

"Do what?"

"Jump like that! You were like a freakin' ninja!"

"Maybe I have secret ninja skills. Ever think of that?"

"I think you're secretly a cat…or something," I muttered, staring at him in disbelief.

He grabbed my hand and shoved the water bottle into it. "Come on. Let's run."

He jogged across the yard but stopped when he reached the blacktop. I was still in the same spot, too confused by what I'd seen to move.

"Are you coming or not?"

I nodded my head and hurried to catch up. Once I was next to him, he started jogging again. The pace was slow enough that I didn't have any trouble keeping up with him—well, at least for the time being.

If he tried to make me run uphill, I knew I wouldn't make it. I wasn't fat or even remotely overweight, but I didn't exercise anymore. I'd spent most of high school as a cheerleader. I'd left the team after everything happened with my mom, and I hadn't bothered to try to stay in shape. I was regretting it now.

Both of us were silent as we jogged down our street and onto the next.

I was still trying to figure out what I'd seen him do back at his house. He'd moved so gracefully and so fast, almost too fast. I thought back to that first day when I'd thought I saw him dent the gym wall with the dodgeball. And he could disappear and reappear without me even noticing. I shook my head. I was going crazy.

I'd been so lost in thought that I wasn't paying attention to where we were jogging. On one of the many one-lane roads in Shinnston, I looked around and realized that we were over a mile away from my house, and we were also in the bad part of town. Sure, several farms were around here, but the area was also known as the place to go to buy drugs.

"Cain, I don't think we should be here," I said, surprised that I wasn't even out of breath. Apparently, I could jog just fine. It was walking uphill that killed me.

"Why not?" He looked over at me.

I wiped sweat off of my forehead, noticing that he wasn't sweating at all. *Ass.* "This isn't a good place to be. People get in trouble out here all the time. Usually, it involves police and less than stellar mug shots."

"I won't let anything happen to you. Don't worry."

"You say that now," I said, glancing around again.

I always avoided this part of town. Even when Jenny and I had been close, I had skipped the parties that happened out here. Every Monday morning, Jenny would fill me in on what had happened, and I'd been glad that I wasn't there.

"Stop freaking out and jog, or I'm going to start sprinting and leave you behind." Cain smirked at me. "I promise you that no one will mess with you as long as I'm around."

I sighed in annoyance but kept my mouth shut. I doubted if Cain would actually abandon me, but I wasn't going to take any chances. We continued to jog, occasionally increasing our speed to a steady run before going back to a jog.

After the first half an hour, I started to feel tired. Cain kept pushing me, refusing to let me quit. I forced him to walk a few times as I tried to keep my breathing under control.

"I need to head back, Cain. I can't go any farther," I said an hour later. It was the truth. I couldn't go any farther, or he'd end up carrying me home or leaving me on the side of the road. Neither option was appealing to me at the moment.

He nodded, and we turned and started walking back the same direction we'd come. It would take us forever to get back, especially since I couldn't jog anymore, but I didn't mind.

Woods and farms surrounded us at this point. We were long past the bad part of town. I watched a farmer maneuvering a round bale of hay into a feeder as the cattle watched him, anxious to start eating. It felt peaceful out here.

I looked up in surprise when Cain rested his hand on my lower back. I was suddenly self-conscious as I realized I was soaked with sweat and probably didn't smell the best. I tensed up, but he didn't seem to notice.

"You did good today, Ella. A lot better than I thought you would. I'm impressed," Cain said.

"We haven't made it home yet. You might not be quite as impressed if you end up carrying me," I joked. "My legs feel like jelly."

"I wouldn't mind," he said quietly.

I glanced at him, expecting to see his usual smirk but it was nowhere to be seen. His expression was serious.

"I'd be dead weight," I said, trying to shake off his strange mood.

"Not at all. In fact, we'd probably make better time if I carried you."

I opened my mouth to reply, but the words died in my throat as he suddenly scooped me up and started jogging. Once I remembered how to speak, I started shouting at him to put me down. He ignored me as he continued to jog.

"Cain! Put me down!" I shouted again as I tried to wiggle free.

His grip on me tightened, but he stopped jogging. I sighed in relief, expecting him to release me.

"I want to do something really stupid right now, Ella," he said, his voice still serious.

I glanced at the pond we were standing next to. "If you throw me in that pond, I will murder you in your sleep!" I shrieked as I wrapped my arms around his neck to keep him from tossing me like a rag doll.

He stared down at me, indecision written across his face. Then, his face relaxed. "Screw the rules," he muttered before doing something I never expected.

He kissed me.

I froze in shock, unable to process what was happening. His kiss wasn't gentle. Instead, I felt like he was trying to devour me. I found myself kissing him back, unable to stop myself. He continued to cradle me in his arms as my hands worked their way into his hair. It was as soft as it looked, and I found myself gently pulling on it, trying to pull his mouth closer to mine as if that were possible.

He hungrily kissed me, like he hadn't kissed anyone in years, like he was trying to make up for lost time. Somehow, I doubted that was the case with Cain. I had no doubt that he'd had girls throwing themselves at him back in Colorado just like the girls here wanted to do. The only thing that had stopped them so far was Jenny's wrath.

He suddenly broke the kiss, looking as shocked as I felt. He released me, and I nearly fell over before finally regaining my balance. I couldn't look away from him. His eyes were closed now, and his chest heaved as if he'd been running nonstop for hours.

My fingers came up and touched my lips. I'd never, ever been kissed like that. I'd had a few boyfriends over the years, and I'd kissed most of them. Not even one of them had come close to Cain in the kissing department.

"Cain, look at me," I whispered.

He shook his head, his eyes still closed.

"Damn it, look at me! What just happened?" I asked.

When he opened his eyes, I froze. The heat of his gaze had me breaking out in sweat for a whole other reason than our jog. I took a step back and stumbled over a pothole in the road. His arm reached out and grabbed me before I fell and embarrassed myself. His touch was like a jolt of electricity running through my body.

"What are you doing to me?" He released me and stepped away.

My mouth dropped open in shock as he started walking down the road again.

What am I doing to him?

I wasn't the one who had kissed him.

I forced my legs to start moving as I tried to catch up to him. When I was walking next to him, I looked over at him. "What was that supposed to mean? I didn't do anything! You kissed me," I said.

"Yeah, I know. Damn it, Ella. I didn't plan that. Nothing has gone according to plan since I got here, and it's all because of you."

"Because of me? I haven't done anything to you." I was confused and hurt by the anger in his tone.

He kicked a piece of gravel. "It isn't supposed to be like this!"

We walked in silence for a few minutes.

Cain obviously had issues, and apparently, impulse control was one of them. I couldn't stop thinking about the way he'd kissed me, so maybe I was just as bad as he was. I didn't understand why kissing me had made him so angry. It wasn't like I'd begged him to kiss me. That was on him. So, why was I on the receiving end of his anger?

"Look, I don't know what happened back there, but let's just—" I started to say, but he hushed me.

"Be quiet." He stopped in the middle of the road. He looked around for a second before he started walking again. "We need to move. Someone's coming."

"How do you know?" I asked.

"I can hear the car. Come on." He started jogging.

I strained my ears, trying to hear. The only sound I heard was his feet hitting the blacktop. I started jogging as well, my legs screaming in protest. I ignored them as I pushed myself harder. It was beginning to get dark, and there was no way I was going to hang out in the middle of nowhere by myself at night.

"Wait up!" I called.

He slowed long enough for me to catch up before increasing his pace again. I groaned in annoyance.

"I don't hear anything. Besides, what does it matter? I hate to break it to you, but we're on a road. Granted, it's a small one, but it's still a road. Cars usually drive on those."

"They aren't friendly," he said.

I could tell by the look on his face that he instantly regretted the words.

"Aren't friendly? Cain, what is going on?" I demanded.

He ignored me as he continued to jog.

A few seconds later, I heard the sound of a car approaching. As it rounded the corner behind us, I glanced back. It was an older model car with a few guys in it. Nothing seemed uncommon about it. Tons of people drove older cars around here.

As the car approached us, it slowed down. I moved closer to the edge of the road, trying to stay out of the way. Cain tensed for a second before falling in line behind me. I slowed to a walk when the car stopped next to us, and one of the guys rolled his window down. I peered inside the car, but I didn't recognize any of the occupants.

I cringed when I caught the smell of weed coming from inside. *Awesome.*

We were on a road that had very little traffic and even less cell service, at dusk, with a carload of stoners. This should end well.

"You two lost?" the guy who had rolled down his window asked.

The other occupants in the car laughed as if he'd said something hilarious.

"No. Just taking a walk," I said, trying to keep my voice cheerful despite the unease I felt.

The guy's eyes landed on me and stayed there. I stared back, willing myself not to be terrified of him or his friends. None of them were that scary-looking as far as I could tell. The one talking looked like he was in his mid-twenties. I could see a few tattoos on his arm, and he had his septum pierced, but that didn't mean he was a bad guy. Tons of people had piercings and tattoos nowadays.

He was attractive, but he had nothing on Cain. The guy's hair was a dirty-blond color, and it was a little shorter than Cain's. His eyes were dark, but I couldn't make out the color in the fading light. He looked a bit skinny, as if he didn't eat that often.

Drug addict, a voice whispered inside my head.

I looked over my shoulder, expecting someone to be standing behind us but no one was there.

Cain stood beside me, his entire body tight with tension. His gaze never left the car in front of us. He could sense that these guys were bad news, too.

"Well, we're on our way to see our friend. He lives a few miles from here. We can give you a ride that far if you want," the man said. "I'm Joe by the way. These are my friends, Andy, Brian, and Seth."

Did he think we were stupid? There was no way I would get into a car with a bunch of guys I didn't know, especially when it smelled like they'd taken a bath in weed.

I shook my head. "No, thanks. We're fine with walking."

"Oh, come on. We won't bite," Joe coaxed.

"Really, we're fine. I appreciate the offer though." I turned and started walking, hoping he would take the hint and leave.

Cain silently followed me. I wondered why he was being so quiet. It wasn't like him at all. Usually, I wanted to shove a sock in his mouth to shut him up.

"Hey, wait a minute!" Joe called as their car started moving.

They coasted beside us as we walked.

I ignored them, hoping that my gut was lying. Right now, it was telling me that I should probably run, or things would end badly for Cain and me. My stomach dropped when I heard the car stop again, and a door opened. I glanced back and saw the guy who had been talking to us climbing out of the car. He moved quickly to catch up. Once he did, he stepped in front of me, blocking my path.

"Why don't you get in the car? We're not going to hurt you," he said.

Liar! the voice shouted in my head. *Run!*

"You're kind of freaking me out by following us. Will you please leave us alone?" I asked, trying to walk around him.

He stepped in front of me, blocking me yet again.

Cain apparently decided it was time to step in. He grabbed me and yanked me back before stepping closer to Joe. "I think you and your friends should move on."

Joe looked Cain over and grinned. "I don't think so. We want to party with your friend." He gestured to me. "You're more than welcome to leave if you want, but she's staying with us." Any kindness in his voice was gone.

I watched him smirk at Cain. He knew Cain didn't have a chance against him and the three other guys in the car. Fear ran through my veins like ice, chilling my entire body. This wasn't going to end well.

"Last chance," Cain said, his face empty of any emotion whatsoever.

Joe laughed. "Or what? I hate to break it to you, but there are four of us and one of you."

Cain shrugged. "I've won against worse odds."

I stared at him in disbelief.

The guy chuckled again before motioning to his friends in the car. My stomach sank even further into a pit of despair as I heard three doors open and close. Before I could blink, they had surrounded us.

"Now, why don't you keep walking?" Joe said to Cain. When Cain didn't move, he frowned. "Suit yourself."

I opened my mouth to shout out a warning when I saw the guy behind Cain lunge for him. My warning wasn't needed—at all. Faster than I'd thought possible, Cain spun and grabbed the guy by his throat. He tossed him across the road like he weighed nothing.

The other two guys jumped toward Cain as one, obviously ticked off over the fact that their friend was lying in a heap across the road. Cain ducked as one of them swung at him. His arm shot out, landing a blow that caused the guy some serious pain. Cain turned to the other guy while the one he'd just hit grabbed his crotch and dropped to the ground, howling in pain. Cain's fist connected with the new guy's face, causing him to fall back. He was a lot bigger than his friends or Cain, and the blow didn't keep him away for long. He ran full force at Cain, head-butting him in the stomach. I watched in horror as the two of them fell to the ground with Cain underneath.

Cain flipped over with what seemed like no effort at all, so the boy was the one pinned underneath. He drew back and slammed his fist into the guy's face. I winced as I heard the sound of his nose breaking. Cain stood and turned just as the first guy leaped at him again. I swore, I had seen Cain rolling his eyes before grabbing the guy and knocking him on his ass.

Joe was staring at Cain in disbelief. It was obvious that he and his goons were rarely put in their place. Anger flashed across his face as he moved toward Cain. Cain, on the other hand, smiled as he watched the guy approach.

Joe was obviously the leader of the group and smarter than the rest. He didn't run at Cain like the others had. Instead, he studied him, looking for a weakness. His eyes fell on me, and he grinned. He lunged toward me, reaching for my arm. He never got the chance to pull me to him though. Cain appeared beside him and slammed his fist into the guy's stomach. The guy's grip on me loosened, and I broke free. I stumbled backward and fell on my butt, scrambling to get away.

Once I was out of the way, Cain unleashed his full fury on the guy. I watched in horror as he landed punch after punch to the leader's face. When the guy stopped fighting back, Cain kicked him in the leg, dropping him to the ground. He gave him one final kick before stepping away.

My heart was racing as I tried to process the scene in front of me. Cain had been jumped by four guys and had won. He didn't have a scratch on him either. How was that even possible?

He crouched down next to the leader and spoke so softly that I almost didn't hear him, "You ever touch her again, and I'll kill you. It doesn't matter though. I'll be seeing you soon enough. I can sense it already. Your nasty little habits are going to be the death of you." He rose and stared down at the guy. "And I promise, I won't hold back the next time we meet."

Cain turned to me. My mouth dropped open in shock as he walked over to me and held out his hand.

He must have noticed the look on my face because his hand dropped to his side. "Ella? What's wrong?" he asked. "You're safe now."

"Your eyes..." I stammered. "They're glowing."

And they were. His eyes were still dark, but they were literally glowing like an animal's eyes in a spotlight.

I froze in horror, unable to process what I was seeing.

Cain instantly closed his eyes and opened them again. The glow was gone.

"How is that possible?" I whispered.

He shook his head. "My eyes aren't glowing, Ella. You're in shock."

He reached down and scooped me up into his arms. While my mind screamed at me to run from him, my body didn't agree. I felt myself relax into him as he carried me.

Neither of us spoke until we reached our block. It was probably the longest Cain had ever been silent in his life. I stared at his eyes, willing them to glow again. I knew what I had seen. There was no way I'd imagined that glow.

"Cain, tell me the truth. Why were your eyes glowing like that?" I finally asked.

"My eyes weren't glowing. That's physically impossible. You were scared because of those guys, and you imagined it." He put me down in the middle of my yard.

"I'm not crazy! I know what I saw!" I shouted. "And how did you do what you did with those guys, Cain? Almost all of them were bigger than you, even the one you tossed around like a rag doll. You shouldn't have won!"

He shrugged. "They were high, Ella, and clumsy."

"You're lying." Anger flooded my brain. "What is going on?"

He turned and started walking toward his house. "Believe what you want. I'm tired, so I'm going to bed. I'll see you tomorrow. Try not to get into any more trouble until then."

I watched as he disappeared inside his house. I didn't move for several minutes, half-expecting him to reappear. When he didn't, I finally gave up and stomped my way across my yard.

I wasn't crazy! I knew what I had seen. He'd taken on four guys and walked away without a scratch. His eyes had glowed.

I wasn't one to believe in the supernatural, but I couldn't help but wonder if Cain was even human. And if he wasn't, then neither was Asher.

That thought chilled me to the bone.

Nine

B y the time Asher knocked on my door at eight, I had showered and made dinner. Unsure of how long Asher planned to stay, I'd even made extra for him. Uncle Jack was running late once again, and I suddenly felt nervous as I walked to the front door to let Asher in.

My uncle trusted me. He'd blatantly told me so on more than one occasion, but I still wasn't entirely sure he would be okay with me having a boy over while he wasn't home—specifically, a boy who looked like Asher.

When I opened the door, Asher was standing there with a smile on his face. I noticed his backpack slung over one arm, full of books. Obviously, he planned to make use of tonight. Strangely enough, that thought brightened my mood.

With Cain, I felt like things could spin out of control at a moment's notice. With Asher, I knew exactly what I was getting—or at least, I thought I did.

"Hey." I smiled at him. "Come on in."

I stepped aside, and he moved past me and into the house. I studied him as he walked by, looking for anything out of the ordinary. I saw nothing, not that I'd really expected to.

Once he was inside, I closed the door behind him and turned. He was standing next to the couch, studying the living room like it was the most interesting thing he'd ever seen.

"What are you looking at?" I asked finally.

He glanced back at me before walking across the room to where Uncle Jack had several of my school pictures hanging on the wall. I instantly felt my face turn red with embarrassment as he studied my fifth grade photo.

"Your house. It's…nice, really nice."

I shrugged. "It's just a house. Yours is way bigger than this one anyway."

He continued to study the photographs on the wall. "It is, but it doesn't have any of *this* in it."

"This?" I questioned.

He finally turned away from the photos and looked back at me. "This house is full of love. One look into this room, and I can instantly see that. Your uncle loves you very much, and it shows."

I thought back to when I had been in his and Cain's house. I remembered that there were no photographs hanging, nothing that made the house feel like a home. "Your mom doesn't like to hang pictures?"

"No, she's never really been one to show either of us off." He seemed uneasy as he pulled his bag off his shoulder. "Where do you want to study?"

I motioned for him to follow me. "I thought the kitchen would be best."

He walked behind me so silently that I glanced back to make sure that he was indeed following me. When we made it to the kitchen, he dropped his bag onto the table.

"I made extra food in case you're hungry. It's chicken," I said. "Would you like some?"

He smiled warmly at me. "Food would be great. Thank you."

I waved him off. "You're welcome. Make yourself at home while I heat it up."

I walked over to the microwave and pushed the buttons to warm the food back up.

Asher sat down at the table and started pulling his books out of his bag. I grinned when I saw both his science and math books laid out. Obviously, he wanted to start with our weaknesses. That was fine with me.

Once the microwave dinged, I grabbed the plate of chicken and mashed potatoes out of it and got a fork from the drawer. Asher moved his books aside as I walked across the kitchen and set the plate down in front of him.

"You want anything to drink?" I asked.

"Water would be good," he said as he picked up his fork.

I grabbed a glass and filled it with water. After setting it down in front of him, I pulled out the chair closest to him and dropped myself down into it. My books were stacked neatly off to one side. I pulled my math book off the top and flipped it open to the page we had been assigned for homework. Asher watched me as he ate.

"I'll go ahead and start on math. When you're done, you can start on the science homework. Then, we'll help each other when we're finished."

"Mmkay." His voice was muffled as he chewed. He swallowed roughly. "This food is amazing by the way. I'm already plotting how I can come over for dinner every night."

I laughed. "No plotting needed. You're welcome anytime. It'd be nice to have company for dinner. My uncle usually gets home late, so I eat by myself a lot."

"I guess you'll be seeing a lot of me from now on then." He smiled.

"You won't hear me complain. Ever since things happened with my mom, I hate being alone."

He hesitated for a minute before speaking, "Can I ask what happened? I've heard a few things at school, but I'd rather hear it from you—I mean, if you're comfortable talking about it."

I studied him. Asher wasn't the type of person to dig for information and then spread it around for everyone to hear. The look of concern on his face was genuine. I knew that without a doubt. For some reason, I trusted not only Asher, but Cain as well. I felt a pull to both of them, something I'd never experienced before. The brothers made me feel safe. They made me feel normal.

I sucked in a deep breath before opening my mouth and spilling everything to Asher, just like I had with Cain. It was strange. I was comfortable telling both of them about my mother, but Amanda— the only person I'd been friends with for months—still had no clue about what had happened. Even if she did ask for the details, I wasn't sure if I would tell her.

After only a few days, Cain and Asher had become safe havens for me. That made me want to question my own judgment. After my mother had betrayed me, trust was not something that came easily for me. I couldn't understand why I could trust the Collins brothers so easily.

When I finished, Asher was quiet for a moment. I shifted uneasily in my chair, looking anywhere but at him. I suddenly feared that he would turn his back on me just like everyone else had.

"I think..." He paused. "I think that everything happens for a reason. Obviously, your mother was unwell. Maybe she misunderstood something she'd heard, and it caused her to lose focus on reality. Maybe by attacking you though, she was finally able to get the help she needed."

"You think a misunderstanding made her try to kill me?" I asked incredulously.

He sighed. "I don't know what I think, Ella. But whatever caused her to snap, I'm sure she wouldn't have done it on her own. She obviously needed help, and she's now receiving it."

"It's too bad that it almost cost me my life though," I said bitterly.

"Life doesn't end in this world, Ella. Our time on Earth is so short when compared to eternity. Losing your life here doesn't mean that everything is over. Sometimes, it's just the beginning."

I raised an eyebrow. "What are you talking about?"

He shook his head. "Never mind. It doesn't matter anyway." He cleared his throat as he pushed his plate aside. "Why don't we work on our homework?"

I watched in disbelief as he opened one of his books and grabbed a notebook. *How could he have changed the subject so abruptly, especially after saying something like that?*

If Asher noticed me watching him, he didn't show it. He kept his attention riveted to his book, never once glancing up at me. Finally, I gave up and turned my attention back to my book. The constant *tick-tock, tick-tock* of the clock above the sink was the only sound in the room. I focused on it, letting the sound soothe me.

We worked in silence for almost half an hour before either of us looked up again.

Asher finished his work first. He stretched his arms above his head. "Can I use your bathroom?"

I nodded. "Yeah. Just go out into the hallway. It's the second door on the right."

"Thanks." He pushed his chair back and stood.

I watched him as he walked across the kitchen and disappeared into the hallway. Once he was gone, I turned my attention back to the math problems in front of me.

Only a few minutes after Asher had left the room, I shivered. I paused for a moment and looked around the empty kitchen before shivering again. The cold only intensified. It suddenly felt like I had stepped into a freezer.

"I hope the stupid air conditioner didn't kick on," I grumbled as I pushed away from the table and stood.

I wrapped my arms around myself to stay warm as I left the kitchen and walked into the hallway where the thermostat was. I stopped in front of the little white box and inspected the digital display.

"Still set at sixty-eight," I mumbled.

Irritated, I made my way to the front door, grabbed one of my lightweight hoodies, and pulled it on. It helped, but I could still feel the chill in the air against my face as I walked back into the kitchen and sat down.

I tried to concentrate on my homework again, but I couldn't. My body started to shake as the cold seemed to press in against me on all sides. It almost felt like a presence was in the room with me, causing the cold.

"Now, you're just being dumb," I said to myself. My eyes widened as I saw my breath as I spoke.

I heard a loud crash come from the bathroom. I froze as footsteps pounded down the hall.

A second later, Asher was standing in the doorway. One look at him was all it took for me to know that something was very, very wrong.

"Asher?" I whispered.

His face was drawn tight in anger…and maybe even fear. I'd never seen him look like that before, and I would be lying if I said that it didn't scare me. He looked terrifying. His beauty was still there, but it was warped in a way that I couldn't explain. The first thought that popped into my mind was that he looked like an avenging angel, the beauty and anger mixing together in one.

He ignored me as he stared at something behind me. I turned to see what he was staring at, but there was nothing. I looked back at Asher. His expression was still terrifying. Add in the fact that his body was shaking so hard that it looked like he was convulsing, and I knew that I needed to get away from him—now.

I started to stand, but I stopped when he held up his hand.

"Don't!" he yelled.

"Asher, what's wrong? Oh my God, you're bleeding!" I gasped as blood slowly started to trickle from his nose.

It changed from a trickle to a gush, running down his lips and chin before dropping to the floor.

Asher closed his eyes as if concentrating very hard. "Cain!" His voice boomed around the room, echoing over and over in my head.

I cringed and closed my eyes, the sound so loud that it almost hurt my ears.

"You called?"

My eyes shot open. Asher was still standing in the exact same spot, but now, Cain was next to him. His words were mild, but his face was set in a determined expression.

"A little help?" Asher demanded.

Without a word, Cain took Asher's hand in his and closed his eyes. Asher's gaze found mine for a split second before he closed his as well.

Within seconds, the cold disappeared from the room. There was no gradual decrease. One moment, I had been shivering with my breath clearly visible, and the next, everything was exactly the same as it had been before.

Cain's eyes opened first. He turned to Asher, who was still shaking with his eyes squeezed shut.

"Asher," Cain said, his voice full of authority. "Asher! Are you all right?"

Asher slowly opened his eyes and pulled his hand free of Cain's. He wobbled for a moment before leaning against the wall. "I'm great. Never been better." His voice was weak.

"What the hell just happened?" I demanded as I stood.

Asher looked over at Cain and gave him a pleading look.

Cain studied him for a moment before looking at me. "Ella, can you grab a towel and a wet cloth, please? Asher's nose is still bleeding."

"I, uh…yeah." I moved around them and went into the hallway.

I dashed into the bathroom and grabbed a towel and washcloth out of the linen cabinet. My hands shook as I held the cloth under warm water. Something…bad had just happened in my kitchen. I had no idea what, but I did know one thing for certain. There was something strange about the Collins brothers. I'd been unsure before when I saw Cain's eyes and the way he fought off those guys, but now, I knew without a doubt that I was right.

I rushed back to the kitchen, but I stopped dead outside the door when I heard Cain and Asher talking quietly. Their voices were muffled, so I moved closer. I stopped just out of sight and held my breath as I tried to hear what they were saying.

"He won't wait much longer," Asher said.

"I know. I can't believe that he's waited even this long."

"What are we going to do?"

"What we came here to do. We have to protect her for as long as possible, or neither of us will succeed," Cain said quietly.

"How are we supposed to do that? You saw what just a few seconds of holding him off did to me. If he came at me again right now, I'd lose."

There was a pause before Cain spoke again, "Then, we'll have to work together—for a little while at least."

Asher snorted. "We've never been good at working together."

"We don't have much of a choice. Her mother's actions set everything into play six months ago. The fact that she's still alive is a miracle."

My mother? I almost gasped out loud, but I caught myself. *What did my mother have to do with any of this?*

"Death is not patient, and he doesn't take sides. We have no choice but to protect her together," Asher said after a moment. He sounded defeated.

Death.

My heart started racing. Unable to stand it any longer, I stepped into the kitchen. The brothers were sitting at the kitchen table, both wearing an identical mask of worry. They turned to me as one, and the worry changed to concern.

"Are you all right?" Cain asked me.

"What are you two talking about?" I demanded. "My mother? Death? *What* is going on?"

Cain stood and stepped closer to me. "I don't know what you're talking about."

"Cut the crap, Cain! Tell me the truth."

He gave me a pitying look as he reached out and gently touched my shoulder. "I'm sorry, Ella."

Then, everything went black.

Ten

When I awoke, everything was black. My chest constricted in fear as I tried to figure out where I was. After a moment, my eyes adjusted to the darkness, and I saw moonlight coming through a window. It was just enough light to realize that I was in my bedroom, lying on my bed.

I slowly sat up and looked around, trying to figure out how I'd ended up here. Suddenly, the scene in the kitchen came crashing back to me—Asher, the coldness, Cain. I shuddered at the memory of the way Asher had looked.

The last thing I remembered was a hushed conversation between the brothers, and then I'd stormed in and demanded answers. Everything had gone black after that. *Maybe I had fainted?* After all, it would be completely understandable to faint after what I'd witnessed.

Obviously, one of them had managed to get me up to my room without any trouble. If Uncle Jack had walked in after I passed out, I was sure his shouting would have woken up even the dead. Still, I needed to make sure that he was okay.

I stood carefully, afraid that my legs would give out on me. I was surprised at how steady they were. In fact, I felt perfectly fine. Carefully, I crossed my room and opened my door. I peeked out into the hallway to make sure Uncle Jack wasn't up before slipping out into the hall and walking to his door. I stopped outside and held my breath, hoping to hear any kind of sound coming from inside.

Finally, after what felt like an eternity, I heard Uncle Jack snoring softly. I was safe.

Now that I knew he was out for the night, I headed back down the hallway to the stairs. I was going to get some answers, and only two people could give them to me. I moved swiftly down the stairs, careful not to step on the stair that creaked, and walked to the front door. I eased it open inch by inch. I slid through the open space and stepped out onto our porch.

After closing the door quietly behind me, I walked across my yard to Cain and Asher's house. Judging from the position of the moon and the lack of lights on our street, I knew it had to be very late—or very early, depending on how I looked at it.

The dead grass crunched with each step. I hurried my pace, not wanting to alert the whole neighborhood to what I was up to. When I reached their front door, I stopped. If I pounded on the door in the middle of the night, I had no doubt that their mother would murder me where I stood. If by some miracle she didn't, Uncle Jack would take care of the job for her.

I finally decided that death by parent wasn't the way I wanted to go. Instead, I stepped off their porch and walked around the side of the house to where I knew Cain's window was. Feeling like a total dweeb, I scooped up a few tiny rocks on my way.

Who throws rocks at windows anymore? We'd simply text. Too bad I didn't have either brother's number.

Once I was below Cain's window, I pulled back and let the first pebble fly. It missed the window by at least a foot. Cursing to myself, I aimed the next pebble and tossed it up. I smiled when it hit the glass. I waited a few seconds to see if Cain would appear before I threw another one. I frowned when he didn't appear at his window.

"You make a habit of throwing rocks at boys' windows in the middle of the night?" a voice asked from right behind me.

I let out a surprised squeal, but a hand quickly clamped over my mouth.

"Don't start screaming, or you'll wake the whole town up at this hour."

The hand released me, and I spun around. Cain was standing only inches away from me. I was surprised that I knew it was him, but I did. Even though I'd only been around him and Asher for a few days, I could finally tell them apart. Cain's stance was different, more rigid, than Asher's. His eyes were sharper, too, whereas Asher's were soft.

"You scared the crap out of me!" I hissed. "What are you doing out here?"

He chuckled. "I could ask you the same thing."

My reason for being in his yard in the middle of the night came to the forefront of my mind. I nodded and motioned toward the front of his house. "We need to talk, and I'd prefer that we didn't do it in the middle of your yard. Can we go inside?"

He shrugged. "Sure, if that's what you want."

I followed him back around to the front of the house. He held the door open for me, and I quickly moved past him and into the safety of his house. I tiptoed into the living room, careful not to trip over anything in the darkness. I winced when he shut the front door, and it closed loudly.

He followed me into the living room, flipping on the overhead light.

"What are you trying to do, let your mom catch me here?" I whisper-shouted.

He chuckled. "As entertaining as that would be, no. She's not home, so there's no need for you to try to be stealthy."

"Oh," I said, feeling dumb. "Where is she?"

"She left town this morning for a business trip. She won't be back for a couple of days."

I sat down on the couch.

Cain dropped down next to me and put his feet on the coffee table. "So, what exactly do you want to talk about?"

"Cain, what on earth are you doing down here? It sounds like you're trying to wake the dead," Asher said as he appeared in the doorway. He froze for a split second when he saw me, but he quickly recovered. "Ella, I didn't expect to see you here in the middle of the night. What brings you by?" He moved across the room toward us.

"She was just about to tell me. Whatever it is, I'm sure it's important. After all, she must be desperate if she was throwing rocks at my bedroom window." Cain grinned over at me. "Not that I'm complaining. But just so you know, there are easier ways to get my attention late at night. We could even work out a flashlight code, so the next time you're so desperate to see me, you won't even have to leave your bedroom. I'll come to you."

His flirty words and tone set me on edge. I was in no mood to get into a bantering competition with Cain at the moment. I'd come for answers, and that was what I was going to get.

I turned to Asher. "I want to know exactly what happened in my kitchen tonight," I said flatly.

Asher's brow creased in confusion. "What are you talking about?"

"Don't play dumb. I want to know what made you act like that and why it suddenly felt like I was living in an igloo." I pointed at Cain. "And, you, I want to know how you knew to show up when Asher needed you."

Cain and Asher looked at each other in total confusion. I wasn't buying it.

"Someone had better start talking, or I'm going to start punching," I growled.

Finally, Cain looked back at me. "I honestly have no idea what you're talking about. I wasn't in your kitchen tonight."

"Don't lie to me!" I shouted, suddenly so angry that I couldn't sit still. I stood and started pacing the room. "I'm not an idiot. I know what I saw!"

Asher spoke up, "Ella, calm down. He's telling the truth. He wasn't with us tonight."

"Then, how did I end up waking up in my own bed when the last thing I remember is the two of you in my kitchen?"

Asher's expression grew more concerned. "We were working on homework tonight, but you fell asleep before we made it very far. I didn't want to leave you passed out on the table, so I carried you upstairs to your room and put you in your bed. Then, I left before your uncle got home, so I could avoid any questions he might ask about why a teenage boy was in your house while you were passed out."

My mouth dropped open in surprise. I'd expected Cain to lie straight to my face but not Asher. I'd always thought of him as the honest one.

"How can you do this?" I whispered. "I thought you were my friend, Asher, yet you can lie to me like this. Hell, if I wasn't one hundred percent sure of what I saw, I'd believe you."

"Ella—" Cain started.

I cut him off, "No, don't, Cain. You two were talking about Death and my mother and something about keeping me alive. I couldn't make something like that up."

Asher moved closer to me, but I backed away. I shook my head at both of them, and then I turned and ran for the front door. I couldn't stand to look at either of them any longer. I'd thought that they were my friends, but obviously, that wasn't the case. Friends wouldn't lie and keep things from each other.

I didn't stop running until I was back on my own porch. I forced myself to breathe in and out as I fought not to cry. If I walked into Uncle Jack's house while sobbing, he'd catch me for sure. I waited until I had calmed down to quietly open the door and sneak inside. After locking the door, I carefully made my way back to my room.

I didn't let myself think about what had happened earlier or my recent confrontation with Cain and Asher until I was lying in my bed, staring up at the ceiling. They'd both lied to me. They had known I wouldn't fall for their trick, yet they had still tried. *Why? What were they hiding that was so important that they couldn't even tell me after what I'd witnessed?*

I'd never believed in the paranormal or anything that was unusual. I had no reason to—until now. Cain's glowing eyes flashed through my mind, followed by his strength. Asher's terrifying expression was next along with the way Cain had magically shown up just when Asher needed his help. Add in the fact that my kitchen had become an ice cube, and I couldn't help but let my mind drift in that direction.

Whatever was happening around me certainly wasn't normal. Nothing in my life had been normal since my mother's attack.

My eyes widened. *My mother.*

The brothers had mentioned her. Obviously, she had something to do with all of this. Since Cain and Asher had refused to tell me what was going on, maybe it was time I finally paid my mother a visit. I closed my eyes. That was something I'd promised myself I would never do. After all the pain and heartache she had caused me, I had sworn that I'd never lay eyes on her.

My hands clenched into fists. "I guess it's time to see each other again, Mom," I whispered, "whether I want to or not."

My mother had answers, answers that I knew I'd never find elsewhere. If I wanted the truth, I would have to face my fears and see her.

My life officially sucked.

Eleven

"I want to visit Mom." That was the first thing I said to Uncle Jack the next morning.

Maybe I should have waited for him to finish taking a sip of his coffee because it took a good five minutes for him to stop choking long enough to speak.

"You what?" he sputtered.

His look of disbelief would have been comical at any other time but not now.

"I want to see Mom. I'm ready." That was possibly the biggest lie I had ever told, but it didn't matter.

"I...I don't understand. I asked you earlier this week to go visit her, and you refused." He paused. "Actually, if I remember right, you stormed out of here at the mere mention of visiting her."

"I know, but I've had time to think. I want to go—today."

Uncle Jack stared at me from across the room, obviously trying to figure out whether or not I'd lost my mind. I shifted my weight from foot to foot, uncomfortable with his gaze.

After what felt like an eternity, he finally nodded. "All right. Let me make a call and see if we can go today."

"Thank you," I said before turning and hurrying out of the kitchen.

It was too late to back out now.

"You're sure about this?" Uncle Jack asked for the fourth time as we headed south on the interstate.

"If you ask me that one more time, I'm going to fling myself out of this car while you're going"—I glanced at the speedometer—"seventy-five miles an hour. And by the way, you're speeding."

He grinned. "Sorry. I just can't get over the fact that you agreed to this. No, actually, I can't get over the fact that you suggested it."

"I need to know why she did what she did to me. That's all."

"Why now?"

I shrugged. "Guess it just felt right."

We stayed silent as Uncle Jack took the exit leading to the hospital. I stared out my window as we traveled along the narrow two-lane road, lost in thoughts of that night.

"Mom, are you home?" I called out as I closed the door behind me.

When she didn't answer, I dropped my bag next to the back door and walked down the narrow hallway of our trailer. The layout was simple, and we'd lived here almost all my life. I could find my way through our home in complete darkness.

I passed my bedroom and the spare room before stopping in the living room. Only a chest-high bar area separated the living room from the kitchen. I saw the top of my mother's head. I sighed. If she was sitting at the kitchen table without answering me, she was probably way past drunk and quickly headed into wasted.

I squared my shoulders in preparation for the fight we would have when I tried to drag her to bed. Resigned to my fate, I moved through the living room, stopping only a few feet from where the kitchen tile began.

"Mom, are you okay?" I asked.

She was facing away from me, but her shoulders tensed, letting me know that she was at least conscious.

Without a word, she stood and walked over to one of the kitchen drawers. As soon as she moved out of the way, my stomach sank. The kitchen table was littered with beer bottles. I knew they were all new since I'd cleaned the house before heading to the football game.

"Mom?" I asked again.

Her silence was starting to bother me. Usually, when she drank, she cried or screamed or threw things. She was eerily calm, and that was somehow worse to me. It was unknown.

My mother pulled something out of the drawer before turning to me. My blood turned to ice when I noticed her eyes. There was absolutely no emotion in them at all. Even worse, they seemed milky, as if she had suddenly developed cataracts while I was at the game.

"Oh my God," I whispered as I fought not to take a step back. "What's wrong with you?"

She smiled, and it chilled me to the bone.

"Ella." My name was nothing more than a hiss on her lips. She stepped closer, the smile never leaving her face.

"I should've known," she said. "I always felt something when you were around me."

She lunged at me, and I screamed as I was knocked off my feet by the force of her impact. I rolled away from her just as she raised her hand. I could finally see what she'd grabbed from the drawer—a knife. I scrambled to my feet as she tried to stab me. I ran around the kitchen table so that it was between us.

"What are you doing?" I shouted.

She stood and turned to me. I was breathing heavily from fear, but she was as calm as she had been when I walked in.

"It's time. The Gods have spoken, and I cannot deny them." She stepped closer.

Only the small space of our table separated us.

"What are you talking about?" I yelled. "Have you lost your damn mind?"

"I've never seen things so clearly in my life." She moved around the table, trying to get closer.

I tripped in my hurry to get away from her. She chuckled as I grabbed the table to steady myself, knocking her beer bottles over.

Without thinking, I picked up one of the bottles by the neck and held it up. "You're drunk. Or you've gone insane! Stop this. I don't want to hurt you, Mom, but you're scaring me."

"They said you have to die tonight. I will not fail them."

"Fail who?" I cried. "You're not making any sense!"

She suddenly darted around the table, surprising me. Her body collided with mine again, and I fell backward. Blinding pain lanced through my skull as my head connected with the cabinets behind me. I fought to stay conscious and fight her off as she tried to pin me to the floor. Her weight pressed down on my ribs, making me feel like I was suffocating.

Terrified, I did the only thing I could do. I swung the beer bottle forward and hit her on the side of the head. She faltered, and I hit her again. Tears streamed down my cheeks as she slowly rolled off of me.

"You're supposed to die," she whispered.

I slammed the bottle against her head one more time, and her body went slack as she passed out.

I stared over at her in disbelief. "Oh my God." I rolled to my knees and hovered over her. "Mom? Mom! Can you hear me?"

I shook her, but her eyes refused to open.

"Help me! Someone, please help me!" I screamed.

Blackness started to take over my vision. The pain in my head intensified, and I slumped over her body.

"Someone help us, please," I whispered before I lost consciousness.

"Ella?"

I pulled myself out of my memories at the sound of Uncle Jack's voice.

"Yeah?" I turned to look at him.

"We're here."

"Oh." I looked out the windshield.

In front of me was a solid-looking wall. A set of black iron gates opened, and Uncle Jack drove through. I studied the wall as we passed. It was a bright white, almost cheerful-looking if it wasn't for the black iron on top. It was meant to look decorative, but I knew from the way it was formed into spikes that it was also meant to keep people out—or in. The wall itself was at least half a foot thick.

As we passed through, I noticed a security house just inside the gate. Obviously, they took security seriously here.

My uncle didn't pay any attention to the wall or the security as we drove down a two-lane road. Up ahead was a building—the hospital. It was made of the same light-colored stone as the wall and was several stories high.

Uncle Jack turned into a parking lot. I kept my eyes on the hospital as he searched for a place to park. All I could think about was that my mother was in there. This was the closest I'd been to her since that night. The fact that I was finally going to see her hit me like a lead ball to the stomach. The car suddenly felt too small, as if all the air had been sucked out of it.

As soon as Uncle Jack parked, I threw my door open and practically crawled out of the car. I squeezed my eyes shut as I tried to keep myself from losing what little control I had.

"Ella, are you okay?" Uncle Jack crouched down next to me and started rubbing my back. "We don't have to do this."

I shook my head as I slowly stood. "No. We're here. I'm not going to turn back now."

He warily watched me as we walked across the parking lot together. When we reached the front doors, they soundlessly slid open. I focused on breathing as I followed him into the building.

The moment I stepped inside, I instantly hated the hospital. The entire décor was based in light colors—white tile floor, cream-colored walls, and white marble counters in the reception area. Several floor-to-ceiling windows were placed across the front of the building. It made the entire area seem calm and open. To me, that made this whole place a lie.

The entire hospital was dedicated to the mentally ill. I'd done my research when my mother was first committed. Several of the patients were criminals who had pled insane. Instead of being sent to prison, they'd managed to snag a one-way ticket here, just like my mother. No, there was nothing happy about this place at all.

Uncle Jack ignored the reception area and walked straight to the elevators. I glanced at the woman behind the desk, who was carefully watching us.

"Uh, Uncle Jack? Do we need to check in?" I asked.

He looked over at the woman. The moment she recognized him, she smiled.

"Hey, Jack. Are you here to see Diane again?" she called.

He waved as he continued to walk. "Yep. I'll see you later, okay?"

He didn't wait for her to respond. He stopped in front of the elevators and pushed the Up button. The doors instantly slid open.

"Come here often?" I asked, half-joking, as we stepped into the elevator.

He pressed the button for the third floor. "Yeah, once or twice a month at least, more if I have time."

"Oh," I said, completely surprised. I knew he'd been here once or twice to see my mother, but I hadn't realized just how often he came here.

"I can't stand to leave her here for long without visiting. I don't want her to think that we've forgotten about her."

Guilt churned in my stomach as the elevator rose, but I ignored it. I had nothing to feel guilty for. My mother was the one who had hurt me. She'd given me absolutely no reason to come here to see how she was.

The doors smoothly slid open, and Uncle Jack stepped out. I followed him as he walked down a hallway to a nurses' station. A pretty redhead looked up from a computer as we approached. She smiled as soon as she saw my uncle.

"Hey, Jack. I'll let Dr. Gralin know you're here," she said.

"Thanks, Lynn," he said before turning to a reception area.

I stayed close as he walked to the nearest chair and sat. I settled in next to him, constantly looking around. Just like the main floor, everything here was bright. The floor-to-ceiling windows were also identical. The sunlight filtered through them, giving the room a cheerful feel.

Less than five minutes later, a doctor appeared. From my sitting position, he looked like a giant. He had to be at least six foot five, maybe taller. His arms were thick with muscles. Obviously, if any of his patients tried something on him, they wouldn't succeed.

While his appearance was a bit terrifying, the smile on his face was warm. His chocolate-colored eyes were soft, kind even. I instantly liked him.

"Dr. Gralin, it's good to see you again." Uncle Jack stood and shook his hand.

"And you as well," he said in a deep voice. He glanced over at me. "And you must be Ella."

I stood slowly and took his outstretched hand. "How did you guess?"

"You look just like your mother."

I frowned at that.

"Follow me, please. We can discuss Diane before you see her." Dr. Gralin turned and headed down a hallway.

Uncle Jack and I followed closely behind him. We stopped at the last door before a set of large doors that appeared to be heavy. They blocked the hallway, and I noticed a keypad mounted to the wall. Obviously, the patient rooms were back there. My mother and others like her were safely locked away behind those doors, away from anyone they wanted to hurt.

Dr. Gralin opened his door and held it for us to pass. Once we were inside, he followed and motioned for us to sit down. Uncle Jack was completely at ease, but I was another story. Each step I took felt robotic, and my movements were jerky.

The doctor sat down in his chair. "I was surprised but glad when Jack called me to ask if you could visit your mother, Ella."

"You weren't the only one," Uncle Jack muttered under his breath, earning a smile from the doctor.

"I'm sure you have a lot of questions about your mother. Ask away." Dr. Gralin leaned back in his chair.

I fiddled with a thread on my jacket. "I'm not sure what I'm supposed to ask, Dr. Gralin. Um, what is she like now?"

The doctor studied me for a moment. "Call me James. And as for your mother..." He paused. "Well, she's made quite the improvement over the last six months. When she arrived, she went through detox, so she's been alcohol-free for her entire stay. That was a huge improvement right from the start. Once she was coherent, we assessed her and started her treatments. She's worked with us almost every step of the way. When you walk into that room, the mother you remember won't be there. Diane's entire demeanor has changed. She's healthy. She's even happy."

"What do you mean when you say she's worked with you *almost* every step of the way?" I asked.

"I've treated your mother since she arrived. I've had private sessions with her along with the group sessions she attends three times a week. We've discussed everything, except for you. She refuses to speak your name or tell me about what really happened that night. When I talked with your uncle last, I suggested that you come to see her. I'm hoping that her interaction with you will allow her to fully open up and take that last step to recovery."

"If she refuses to talk about me, then how do you know that she won't go after me like before?" I demanded.

He sighed. "We don't. But we will have two staff members inside the room with you at all times. If she does try to attack you, they will immobilize her. You don't have to be afraid, Ella."

"That's reassuring," I grunted.

"Ella," Uncle Jack said, his voice sharp.

"Sorry," I mumbled.

"It's okay. I understand that you're nervous, and you have every right to be, but we'll be with you through all of this. I truly believe that your presence is needed for her to continue on the right path. She has faced many of her demons, and dealing with what she did to you will keep her on the right track."

I took a deep breath. "Fine. Can I see her now?"

He nodded. "Yes, we already have her in an isolated visiting room. She knows you're coming, and she's waiting."

I stood. "Then, let's go. We wouldn't want to keep Mommy waiting."

Dr. Gralin frowned, but he didn't comment on my crappy attitude. Instead, he stood and walked to the door. Uncle Jack shot me a glare before following him. I had no doubt that he'd give me a stern lecture when we made it back to the car.

I followed them out of Dr. Gralin's office and to the locked double doors. The doctor entered a code, and they slowly swung open. Another nurses' station was just inside the doors. Two male nurses sat behind desks. As soon as they saw Dr. Gralin, they stood and silently followed us down a hallway. We stopped outside a door. Next to it was a large glass window made of one-way glass.

One of the nurses unlocked the door and stepped inside. Uncle Jack gave me an encouraging smile, and I followed the nurse inside. Out of the corner of my eye, I saw the second nurse fall in line behind me.

The room was small with only one table and two chairs. There were two overhead fluorescent lights but no windows. My mother was sitting at the table with her back facing me.

I stopped, the night in our trailer flashing through my mind. When I'd come home, she'd been sitting the exact same way. Déjà vu was not something I wanted to experience right now.

One of the nurses walked to the far wall and turned around so that he was facing my mother. The other stood next to the door, directly behind her.

I inhaled deeply, filling my lungs with air, as I slowly crossed the room. I walked around the table without looking at her. When I reached the chair across from her, I sat down. It took less than five seconds, but to me, it felt like an eternity.

Finally, I looked up. My blue eyes instantly met her identical pair. Her eyes were normal again, not the emotionless milky ones I remembered from that night. She'd gained weight, something that she had desperately needed. Her face was no longer sunken in. Her dark brown hair was longer and much better cared for than I was used to. She looked healthy. She looked sane. It took everything in me not to turn away from her.

"Ella." Her voice was soft.

"Mom." I kept my tone indifferent.

We studied each other for a few moments.

"I see you're not lunging across the table to attack me this time. I guess the doctor was right. You have improved."

Without a doubt, I knew that Uncle Jack would tell me off for that one, but I couldn't help it.

"And I see that you're still alive. I guess we're both surprised."

"What's that supposed to me?" I demanded.

She shook her head. "It doesn't matter."

"Oh, but I think it does. I mean, the fact that I'm breathing is what brought us both to this room, so please enlighten me as to why you are surprised that I still have a pulse."

She glanced at the nurse behind me, but she stayed silent. Her eyes flashed to mine. I perfectly understood what she wanted—for us to be alone. I carefully studied her, looking for any signs that she was about to attack me. She remained calm. Truthfully, I couldn't think of a time I'd ever seen her so calm.

"I'd like to speak to my mother—alone," I said, my decision made. I wanted answers, and I knew there was no chance she'd give them to me if these two men stayed with us.

"Miss, I don't think that's a good idea," the nurse behind my mother said.

"It's fine. You're not going to hurt me, are you, Mom?"

She gave me a smirk but didn't speak up.

"Seriously, guys, give us a moment."

Both men seemed to hesitate before the one I could see finally nodded. "If you need us, we'll be right outside."

I waited until they closed the door behind them before speaking to my mother again, "We're alone, so start talking. Why are you surprised that I'm still alive?"

"Because Death marked you. They told me so. I thought they'd send someone else since I'd failed."

I gave her an incredulous look. "Who's *they*?"

"The Gods," she said simply.

Goose bumps rose across my skin. Whatever the doctor thought he knew, he was wrong. My mother wasn't any closer to passing the sane mark than she had been the night of the attack.

"And how do you know what they want?" I asked.

If it wasn't for what had happened with the brothers, I would've walked out of the room without another word, but now, I had to know what my mother wanted to tell me.

"They spoke to me that night while you were at the game." She smiled. "*It all begins when she ends.*' They made it clear that your time was up, and it was my responsibility to end your life, so you could continue on to the next one."

"You do realize how crazy you sound right now, don't you?" I asked.

"Of course I do, but it doesn't matter. They spoke to me. I just don't understand why they've left you alone for this long…unless…"

"Unless what?"

Her eyes narrowed. "Either something is protecting you, or they meant what they said to me. It's *my* responsibility to end you."

I pushed my chair away from the table. "I've heard enough. I'm leaving now. Have a nice life, Mother." I stood and walked around the table, careful not to turn my back on her.

"Ella?" my mother said softly as she turned to face me when I reached the door.

"What?" My hand gripped the doorknob. All I wanted was to escape this room.

"I love you. I hope you know that. You're destined for great things. You'll end this war and save so many."

Her words floored me. *"I love you."* She had a funny way of showing it.

I was so shocked that I didn't even see her lunge for me. One minute, I was standing there, and the next, I was on the floor with my mother on top of me. Her hands circled my neck, choking off my air supply. I fought for breath that would never come as my hands closed over hers. No matter how hard I pried, her grip refused to loosen.

Our bodies were pressed up against the door, blocking the nurses, doctor, or my uncle from getting into the room. I felt the door banging against my hip over and over, but they couldn't get in.

My eyes locked with my mother's again. Instead of the emptiness I'd expected, I saw regret.

"I'm so sorry that I have to do this to you," she whispered.

My struggles lessened as black spots danced in front of my eyes, but I fought to stay conscious. If I closed my eyes, without a doubt, I knew that I'd never open them again.

No, I thought, *I won't die like this!*

With one last bout of energy, I bucked my hips. She was still on top of me, but her grip loosened just a fraction—enough to give me hope. My head shot forward, my forehead connecting with hers. She cried out in pain as she rolled off of me.

With her weight gone, the nurses could finally get the door open. They rushed into the room, followed by the doctor and my uncle. The look of pure horror on Uncle Jack's face was the last thing I saw before I passed out.

Twelve

As soon as I opened my eyes, I almost instantly closed them again. A bright fluorescent light was attached to the ceiling directly above my head, blinding me. I slowly peeled my eyes open again, giving them time to adjust to the brightness. As soon as they were open, I instantly knew where I was—a hospital room. I'd woken up in one just a few months ago after my mother's attack.

I snorted out loud. Of course she was the reason I was in one again.

I reached up and touched my throat, wincing as my fingers made contact with the sensitive skin there. Without a doubt, I knew that I would have two hand-shaped bruises circling my throat.

The door to my room swung open, and I looked up. Uncle Jack walked in. The moment he saw that I was awake, he rushed over to me.

"Ella, are you okay?" he asked.

"I'm fine." I winced at the sound of my voice. I sounded like an eighty-year-old chain smoker.

"I'm so sorry. I never should've agreed to bring you here. I thought—"

"It's okay." I kept my voice at a whisper. "You didn't know what she'd do."

"It doesn't matter! I was so focused on helping her that I never even thought she'd do something like that." He faltered. "Through that window, I watched her attack you, Ella, and there was nothing I could do to stop it. I knew what she'd done last time, but seeing her actually hurt you, I...I can't grasp it. My sister isn't a violent person. She never has been."

"She thinks she's doing the right thing," I said, still keeping my voice low. "She thinks some higher power is telling her what the right thing is."

"What are you talking about?" Uncle Jack asked.

"Before she attacked me, that's what she said. She thinks the Gods are talking to her. She really believes that she's doing the right thing by trying to kill me. The first time, she wasn't herself. I could've looked past it, but this time, she was fine. She told me she loved me." I laughed humorlessly. "I saw her face when she was on top of me. Her expression was full of regret."

"She's insane," he said after a moment. "Totally and completely insane!"

"She is," I agreed. Or at least, I thought she was.

My reasons for finally seeing her came back to me. So many things she'd said were similar to Cain and Asher's conversation.

"Death marked you."

Hadn't they mentioned Death, too?

But while they seemed determined to protect me, my mother obviously didn't agree.

"I just don't understand why they've left you alone for this long…unless…"

"Unless what?"

"Either something is protecting you, or they meant what they said to me. It's my responsibility to end you."

She thought that maybe someone was protecting me. *Could it be possible that she was right? Could two teenage boys be the reason I was still alive?*

It was ridiculous to think about, but right now, every option was possible.

I'd come to my mother for answers, but the only thing she'd managed to do was leave me with more questions.

"I promise you one thing, Ella. You will *never* see your mother again. I'll make sure of it," Uncle Jack said, pulling me from my thoughts.

"That's much appreciated," I mumbled. "When can I get out of here?"

"I'm sure Dr. Gralin will want to check you over again, but after that, we should be able to leave."

"Good," I said.

It was time to find the answers I was looking for, and my first stop would be on Cain and Asher's doorstep.

Despite my protests, the doctor kept me overnight just for observation. I was pretty sure he thought I might sue the hospital for leaving me alone with my mom.

Early the next morning, I was in the process of being released from the hospital.

Dr. Gralin thoroughly checked me over, constantly apologizing for what my mother had done. I ignored him, my mind too focused on what Cain and Asher were hiding from me.

Once I was given the okay, he let me go. Besides the bruises on my neck and my gravelly voice, my mother had done no permanent damage. I was relieved. I was also smart enough to know that if I hadn't been able to get her off of me when I did, I would be dead right now.

The ride home was uncomfortable. Uncle Jack tried to keep up a steady flow of conversation, but it was kind of hard when I refused to participate. Finally, he just gave up and stayed quiet.

The silence gave me time to think, not that it did me much good. I needed to find a way to get the brothers to confide in me, but I had no clue how. That made me angry. Whatever was going on, it had to do with me, so I had a right to know.

By the time we pulled into our driveway, I had moved on from angry to furious. No matter what argument I thought about using, I knew none of them would work. The only thing I was sure of was that I had a better chance of finding out the truth from Asher than I did with Cain. Even though Asher had lied to me, I knew he was the more honest one of the two. Cain would just sidestep my questions with sarcasm or outright lie to me. Somehow, I had to make Asher trust me enough to give me the truth.

Guilt churned in my stomach. I liked Asher, I truly did, but I knew that anything I did from this moment on would be laced with untruths. Every kind word I said or action I made would be to gain his trust. To me, that wasn't true friendship. I would only be using him.

It's to protect yourself. I had to remind myself over and over again.

I wouldn't be doing anything that would truly hurt Asher. I just needed answers.

As soon as Uncle Jack shut off the car, he was out and walking around to my door. He opened it for me, and I climbed out. Worry was still etched into every line of his face. I fought not to roll my eyes. He'd been the same when I first came to live with him. It had taken almost two months for him to finally realize I wasn't going to have a breakdown of my own. After witnessing my mother's second attack, I was sure it would take him longer than two months this time.

I glanced over at Cain and Asher's house as I crossed my yard. It looked empty, no light or movement coming from any of the windows. I knew better. From somewhere inside, one of them was watching me. I could feel it.

"You can't hide forever," I whispered before walking into Uncle Jack's house.

I spent the rest of the day locked in my room. I was supposed to work at the theater that night, but I called in sick. There was no way I could handle dealing with the general public all night. Plus, we were required to wear a uniform at work. They'd never allow me to wear a scarf to hide the bruises on my neck.

Instead of working, I took a quick shower and settled in for the evening. I could've worked on some of my homework, but I decided against it. It was Sunday, but school was closed tomorrow for a holiday. I considered that to be the only bit of luck I'd had lately. I wasn't sure how I was going to hide my bruises until they faded, but at least I had another day to myself.

I shut off my bedroom lights and crawled into bed. I pulled the sheets up to my chin and snuggled down into them until I found a comfortable position. Even though I was exhausted both mentally and physically, I couldn't fall asleep. I tried to clear my mind, but no matter what I did, my thoughts continued to drift back to the brothers. Everything had changed so quickly between us.

For a moment, I considered the fact that maybe, just maybe, I had imagined all of it. I knew that wasn't true. The things I'd seen could possibly be explained as something normal if they didn't occur so close together. Cain's eyes and his strength had been the first signs that something wasn't right, but I could've pushed that aside if it weren't for the fact that they had occurred right before things had happened in my kitchen.

I felt insane. My every thought made me believe that Cain and Asher weren't normal teenage boys. I wasn't even sure they were human. That thought scared me. What if I was losing my grip on reality? What if whatever sickness my mother had was being passed down to me?

That was the last thought I had before I slipped into unconsciousness.

When I awoke, it was still dark in my room, the only light coming from the moon shining through my window. I slowly sat up and rubbed my eyes, wondering what had caused me to wake up. Usually, when I fell asleep, I would sleep like the dead until my alarm went off.

I glanced at my phone, noting that it was just after two in the morning. I sighed. Of course it was. Two o'clock, and I was wide awake. I probably wouldn't go back to sleep for hours.

A gentle breeze moved through my room, brushing my hair away from my face.

I froze. Why would there be a breeze in my room? I knew for certain that my window had been locked before I went to bed. Preparing myself for whatever I would see, I turned and looked at my window. It was open with the curtains billowing around it.

"What the hell?" I whispered as I stood and walked over to it.

I looked down into my yard, almost expecting to see someone moving around, but there was nothing. Still, the open window unnerved me. I slid it shut and locked it. I even pulled up on it to make sure that it was indeed locked.

Shaking my head, I turned back to my bed and stopped dead. Someone was sitting on my bed.

Before I could make a sound, the light on my nightstand clicked on. I blinked. The person on my bed hadn't moved an inch.

"Evening, Ella."

I stood up straighter. "Cain. Can I ask, what are you doing in my bedroom in the middle of the night?"

"I was in the neighborhood. Thought I'd stop by."

I should've screamed for Uncle Jack. In fact, if I were smart, that would've been the first thing I did when I saw that someone was in my room. But I wasn't smart, not when it came to the Collins brothers. Having Cain in my room should have terrified me, especially after what I'd witnessed, but it didn't. Some part of me knew that he wouldn't hurt me.

"And you used my window to visit." It wasn't a question but a statement. "Let me guess. I can add wall-climbing to your abilities."

He chuckled. "What abilities?"

"Strength. Glowworm eyes. A knack for knowing when your brother needs your help. And before you ask, no, I don't know exactly what it was you helped him with. I'm still trying to figure that part out, but…" I paused. "I know it has something to do with Death."

If I'd expected him to react, I would be sadly disappointed. All he did was watch me with that smirk of his on his face.

"You can tell me what's going on, what you and Asher are protecting me from. I won't freak out," I said when he didn't speak up.

"I know for a fact that you would indeed freak out if you knew even half of the truth, Ella." He gave me a pitying look. "Sometimes, it's better to just let things go."

"You have no idea how I'd react. Maybe I'm stronger than you think," I shot back. "Besides, it isn't your place to decide what I can and cannot handle."

"Oh, but it is. And as for your ability when it comes to dealing with the truth, I assure you, I know how you'd react and the outcome."

I studied him. "How could you possibly know that?"

He walked over to me. I stood my ground. If I backed away from him, I knew it would only make him think he was right about me. I would not show fear, no matter what.

"I've seen it time and time again." He looked almost sad. "I've felt it."

"What are you talking about?" I whispered.

He was so close that I could feel his breath against my face. It unnerved me to have him so near, especially after the last few days.

If he noticed my discomfort, he ignored it and stepped closer, effectively removing the small space that had been left between us. He softly smiled at me before lowering his lips to mine. My breath caught in my throat as he gently kissed me. I was so shocked that it took me a moment to respond.

Before I could think about what I was doing, I wrapped my arms around his neck and pulled him closer. Kissing him like this was even better than the first time. I wanted to lose myself in him.

I was so engrossed in our kiss that I didn't notice the chill that slowly started to seep into my room. By the time I felt it, it was too late. Cain seemed to feel it at the same time I did. He jerked away from me and looked to his left. His eyes started to glow again as a look of anger flashed across his face.

I was so mesmerized by his eyes that it took me a moment before I could look away. I'd known that they could do that, but to see it again was still shocking. The only thing I could think was that I officially had proof that everything I'd seen before was real.

Finally, I managed to follow his gaze to the corner of my room. It was empty, but as I stared, the temperature dropped even more. I shivered as I willed my eyes to see whatever was in the room with us.

Cain sucked in a shocked breath. "No!"

Before I could ask what was wrong, he flew backward. I watched in horror as he was thrown across my room. A choked cry escaped me when he reached my wall. Instead of crashing into it, he went *through* it. I scrambled across the room to where he'd disappeared. The wall was still intact, but Cain was nowhere to be seen.

A sound filled the room. I wasn't completely sure what it was, but it sounded like a rustling cloak. I fought not to fall to the floor as the cold became more intense. It was almost overpowering.

My teeth chattered as I slowly turned around. A cloaked figure stood only inches away from me. I let out a shriek as I stumbled back against the wall, desperate to escape. The figure moved closer until we were nearly touching. The craziest thing was that I couldn't see it clearly even though it was practically on top of me. All I could see was a dark shape covered by a black cloak. It was as if I were looking through water. The image was distorted and lacked any real detail.

"*Oriskany.*" A distorted voice filled the room.

It reminded me of water as well. The sound was like I was hearing something while under water.

"What?" I stuttered.

The figure remained in front of me for a moment longer before it gradually faded away right before my eyes. As soon as it disappeared, the temperature in the room returned to normal. I stared at the spot it had stood in, willing it to come back to explain who or what it was while also willing it to never show itself to me again.

I started to take a step forward, but the room suddenly started to dissolve around me. The walls started to melt slowly to the floor, leaving nothing but darkness in their place.

I gasped and sat straight up in bed. My lungs burned as I tried to suck in enough oxygen. I couldn't. I felt like I was drowning. I pulled my knees up to my chest and rested my head against them. I closed my eyes as my body started to shake uncontrollably.

It took a while, but I was finally calm enough to open my eyes again. I looked around my room, expecting to see melting walls and shadowy figures. Not a single thing was out of place.

"It was just a dream," I whispered.

It didn't *feel* like a dream. It felt real, far too real for comfort.

I remembered Cain's appearance and instantly jumped out of bed to run to the window. When I reached it, the window was firmly locked. I quickly unlocked it and lifted it. A cold breeze filled my room, causing me to start shivering again.

I looked down to the yard below my window. I half-expected Cain to be lying there, broken. There was nothing. I sighed and rested my forehead against the glass.

"I'm going crazy. There's no other option," I muttered.

I stood like that until the cold air became too much. I moved my head away from the glass and reached up to pull the window back down. Once it was closed, I locked it. Still wondering if I was going crazy, I took one last look outside. I stilled when I saw Cain standing in his own window, staring right at me. His body was shaking. I could tell that from even this far away.

He silently watched me, never once smirking. He looked as shaken up as I felt. I backed away from the window, my eyes never leaving his.

When I was far enough away, I turned and ran to my bed. I climbed in and pulled the covers over my head, hoping to shut out the world.

I knew one thing for sure. If he was as unnerved as I was, then it wasn't just a dream.

Thirteen

The next morning, I was up and dressed as soon as the sun rose. I'd tried in vain to sleep after Cain and the cloaked figure had paid their visits, but I hadn't been able to close my eyes for more than a few minutes. I'd kept replaying my conversation with Cain over and over, wondering if I really was going crazy and imagining things. Somehow, I didn't think so. Whatever had happened last night, it was real. I'd *really* watched Cain's eyes glow. I'd seen an invisible…*something* toss him across the room before he went through a solid wall. That same something had spoken to me. It had said just one word, but I'd heard it clearly.

"Oriskany."

For some reason, that word sounded familiar, but I couldn't figure out why. I knew that I'd heard it before. The memory teased me, hiding just out of my grasp. Annoyed with myself, I did the only thing I could do. I grabbed my laptop and searched for the word online.

When the search results loaded, I stared at the screen, completely surprised. At least I knew where I'd heard the word before—history class. Oriskany wasn't the name of a person, like I'd expected. Instead, it was the name of a battle, one fought over two hundred years ago in the state of New York. I skimmed through the information on the battle, wincing at some of the facts.

"One of the bloodiest battles of the Revolutionary War," I read out loud. That was cheerful—not.

I opened link after link, trying to understand why that...*thing* would want me to look up a battle that had taken place so long ago. It made absolutely no sense. Still, I continued to click on article after article, hoping that something would stand out.

After almost forty-five minutes of rereading the same information over and over, I was about to give up. I groaned as I clicked on one more article. I scrolled down the page, ignoring the information I'd already seen. When I reached the bottom of the page, there was a link to a list of the soldiers who had died in the battle. I clicked on it, more out of morbid curiosity than anything.

A plain white page appeared with a list of names. I read through them. About halfway down the list of Patriots, I stopped. My mouth hung open in shock.

Cain Collins, Johnstown.

I blinked and rubbed my eyes, almost expecting the name to disappear. It didn't.

My heart started beating faster as I continued to read down the list of deceased Patriots, looking for Asher. I let out a sigh of relief when I reached the end. He wasn't on there.

I scrolled further down the page, skimming over the list of Indians who had died before reaching the list of Loyalists. It was much shorter than the list of Patriots. I carefully read each name, not wanting to miss one. When I read the last name, my hands clenched into fists.

Asher Collins, Johnstown.

I scrolled back up the page and found Cain's name again. I reread it twice before going back to Asher's.

"This can't be possible," I whispered. "The battle of Oriskany was fought in 1777."

I tried to tell myself that these men were Cain and Asher's ancestors. Under any other circumstances, I could have believed it, but I knew that wasn't the case. The cloaked figure wouldn't have given me the name if these two men were nothing more than long forgotten family members.

Cain and Asher were alive in 1777. That realization was enough for me to let my laptop slide off my lap. Then, I realized something even worse. Not only had they been alive then, but according to this article, they had died in 1777 as well.

Cain and Asher had died. Yet, here they were, over two hundred years later, living next door to me.

I knocked on Cain and Asher's door an hour later. I had printed off the list of names, and I now tightly gripped it in my shaking hands. I kept waiting for the shock to wear off, but it didn't seem to be going anywhere. I was knocking on the door of two dead men. That wasn't normal. Nothing about my life had been normal since they moved in. It had only been a week since they stormed into my life, but it felt like years.

The door swung open. I took a step back when I saw one of them standing there. I studied him for a moment, deciding that it was Asher.

"Ella? What are you doing here?" Asher asked, obviously surprised to see me standing on his doorstep so early in the morning.

"We need to talk," I said, hoping that he couldn't hear the fear in my voice.

"Okay…" He moved aside and motioned for me to come in.

I moved past him, careful not to let an inch of my skin touch his. He seemed to notice that.

He frowned as he closed the door. "What's going on?" he asked.

"Where's Cain?"

"Upstairs, I think."

I walked to the bottom of the staircase. "Cain! Get down here!" I shouted loud enough to wake the dead—pun intended.

"Ella? What's wrong?" Asher asked.

I ignored him. I wanted both of them in the same room for this. I wasn't going to let them lie their way out of this. I was going to learn the truth even if a part of me didn't want to know.

"What's with all the shouting?" Cain grumbled as he appeared at the top of the stairs.

He slowly started walking down. His hair was messy, as if he'd just awoken. Judging by the sweatpants and T-shirt he was wearing, I guessed I really had forced him to crawl out of bed.

"Some people actually like to sleep in," he said when he reached the bottom of the staircase.

"You can sleep later," I said.

I wanted to tell him he would've had more sleep if he wasn't creeping into my room in the middle of the night, but I kept silent.

Instead, I turned and walked over to the living room. I stood awkwardly in the center of the room, unsure of what to say now that I had their attention. Both of them moved in closer. I almost took a step back to get away from them, but I caught myself at the last second.

"I want the truth—all of it," I finally said.

Cain rolled his eyes. "Are you seriously still going on about this? Whatever you think you saw wasn't real. It was a dream, Ella. That's all. You fell asleep when you were studying, and you had a nightmare."

"Stop lying!" I growled as I held up the papers I'd printed off. "We all know that I'm not crazy, and I wasn't dreaming." I paused to glare at Cain. "I wasn't dreaming that night, and I definitely wasn't dreaming last night."

"Last night?" Asher's voice was guarded.

"Yeah, last night, when Cain paid me a visit in the middle of the night. Only his visit was cut short when someone else decided to join the party."

"What on earth are you talking about?" Cain asked.

I laughed, but it sounded crazy. "You're such a good liar, Cain, but I'm not buying it."

"Who else was there?" Asher asked. He wasn't looking at me any longer. Instead, his eyes were glued on Cain.

"No one was there, not me and definitely not anyone else!" Cain said angrily.

"I don't know who it was. He was in a black cloak. I watched him throw Cain through a solid wall, a wall that he passed right through."

"A cloaked figure?" Asher whispered. His tan skin had visibly paled. "And you saw him?"

I nodded. "I not only saw him, but he spoke to me."

It was Cain's turn to go pale.

"Aren't you guys curious about what he said?" I asked.

Neither of them said a word.

I took that as my cue to continue speaking, "He said only one word—Oriskany. Does that mean anything to either of you?"

Asher was changing from pale to green. "Ella—"

I shook my head. "Don't try to talk your way out of this. I did some research this morning. You'll never believe what I found."

I held out the papers so that Cain could read them. Asher moved closer so that he could see what was on them as well. I waited as they read down through the names.

"That's a list of all the men who lost their lives in the Battle of Oriskany. You're both on it," I said.

Asher peeled his eyes away from the papers to look at me. He started to move closer, but I held up my hand to stop him.

"No. This ends now. I want to know what or who you really are." I glanced at Cain. "I want to know who both of you are."

The brothers briefly glanced at each other. Asher looked worried, but Cain only smirked.

"Tell her, brother. She deserves to know," Cain said as he sat down in one of the living room chairs. "I can't wait to hear your version."

Asher's eyes darted back and forth between Cain and me. He was no longer green, but his skin was still pale. "I can't. They gave me rules. Telling her the truth isn't allowed. There will be consequences."

"Screw the consequences! I'm tired of being lied to. Tell me everything!" I shouted.

"If you won't do it, I will, brother," Cain said, his cocky nature returning.

Asher sighed. "As you wish. Ella, I think you need to sit down. What I have to say isn't something a person should ever hear while standing up."

I snorted but backed up and sat down on the couch. "I'm sitting. Talk."

He sat down on the opposite side of the couch, leaving me directly between the brothers. It seemed like that was where I always was.

"What do you know of Heaven and Hell?" Asher asked.

I snorted again. "Really? You want to know if I'm religious?"

161

"Just answer the question."

"I know that Heaven is where God is. People who are good go to Heaven when they die. It's filled with clouds and angels and happiness. The Devil controls Hell. When someone is evil, that's where they end up. The Devil and his demons torture them for eternity."

Cain chuckled, earning a glare from Asher.

"I want you to listen to me very carefully, Ella. Everything you just told me? I want you to wipe it from your mind. What I'm about to tell you will change everything for you," Asher said.

"All right," I said slowly, wondering where on earth he was going with all of this.

"Heaven and Hell *do* exist, but it's not like the Bible says. Instead of…clouds and fire, they're simply alternate realms. Both look much like Earth. Each place is ruled by a council of five—one Leader and four lessers who help the leader keep control. The leader's vote holds more power than the lessers, but they can overrule the Leader if it comes to that. I can't think of a time when they've ever fought their leader," Asher said.

"Are you kidding me right now? You really expect me to believe this?" I asked.

"He's telling the truth. Just let him explain everything before you start calling us liars—again," Cain said from the chair.

I opened my mouth to tell him off, but I closed it and nodded. "Fine. Continue, Asher."

"Thank you. Anyway, the leaders are what I suppose you would consider God and the Devil, but they don't go by those names. The leader of Heaven has many names, but lately, she goes by Charmeine."

Cain snorted, and Asher glared at him.

"What?" I asked.

"In angel lore, Charmeine is a name of an angel who brings harmony, but I can assure you that *Charmeine* doesn't want harmony," Cain said.

Asher continued to glare at him for a moment before continuing, "The leader of Hell currently goes by the name of Joseph. Long ago, before your Bible was written, before man overran the Earth, Heaven and Hell were the same place. Charmeine and Joseph ruled together over the souls of mankind. I don't know exactly what happened, but they turned bitter toward each other. They fought. In the end, they split Heaven and Hell into two realms instead of one. Joseph took souls that were damaged, and Charmeine took the souls of those who were pure.

"As mankind's population grew, the leaders could no longer handle the realms on their own. This was when the lessers were created. Both Charmeine and Joseph took the four oldest souls in their worlds and gave them powers similar to their own, only less of them—hence the name, lessers. That worked for a long time, but once again, mankind's population grew to the point where the leaders and lessers could no longer handle them.

"Charmeine and Joseph created armies from the souls they watched over. These souls became what you call angels and demons. They too have powers, but they're not as strong as the leaders or even the lessers. They are tasked with the job of watching over and commanding the souls as the councils and leaders see fit. It is also their responsibility to lead souls to Heaven and Hell once they leave Earth."

"I'm actually impressed with you, Asher. You know your history," Cain teased. "Except for one very important fact that you haven't mentioned. As time went on and the Earth changed, the souls changed. No longer were there strictly pure and strictly evil souls. Yes, there are still some who are truly pure and truly evil, but most of the souls now are tainted. The pure souls have some evil in them, and the evil souls often have purity buried deep inside."

"I was getting to that, Cain." Asher glared over my head at him.

"My bad. Continue," Cain said as he grinned.

Asher rolled his eyes. "Once the souls became tainted, the angels' and demons' jobs became trickier. Before, they knew exactly which souls to bring back to their respective realms, but now, it is the soul's choice in most cases. If a rare soul is still completely pure or completely evil, then it's easy. But the reality is, the armies are tasked with the job of bringing back pure or evil souls along with trying to convince tainted souls to come with them as well."

"But why?" I asked, unable to stop myself.

They were both full of poo, but their story was entertaining.

"Because Heaven and Hell are at war. Charmeine and Joseph each want to control both realms. The souls they collect are their soldiers in battles. The angels and demons are like their generals."

"I don't understand," I said.

"It's simple. Charmeine and Joseph are the original souls. They are the beginning of everything. But they are also both tainted souls. They are both good, yes, but they also have *unsavory* qualities as well. Neither is willing to give up their realm, but they both want more. The war they're fighting has been raging on for thousands of years. Sometimes, Hell has the upper hand, and other times, Heaven does. But that's all about to change," Cain said quietly.

Asher looked like he wanted to argue with Cain's statement, but he didn't.

"What's going to change?"

"Do you know what prophecies are?" Asher asked.

"Um, yeah. They're things that are supposed to happen in the future, right? Like when someone has a vision of what is to come."

"You're exactly right. A prophecy now says a soul will join the battle soon. This soul will be the one who changes everything. Whichever side this soul chooses, that side will win. Once Heaven or Hell wins, either Joseph or Charmeine and their council of lessers will be stripped of their powers. They will become just a normal soul, controlled by the winning side." Cain explained.

"Why will this soul change everything?" I asked.

"Because the soul will have the Touch of Death. Once in the realms, anyone this soul touches will die or lose all of their abilities, depending on how strong the soul is. And there's no coming back from Death in Heaven or Hell. Your soul is just gone. The soul's touch won't kill the lessers or Charmeine or Joseph, but it will strip them of their powers. At least, we don't think it'll kill them." Asher said.

"What kinds of powers do the leaders, lessers, angels, and demons have?" I asked.

"Several, but just to name a few—speed, strength, traveling between the realms and Earth. Angels and demons are usually invisible on Earth by choice, but they can also change their appearance to whatever they want, and they can enter dreams. Like I said, the powers lessen with each chain of command. The leaders are the strongest, then lessers, and then the angels and demons. Souls themselves have none of these powers unless they're chosen to be an angel or demon," Cain said.

I looked back and forth between the two brothers. They never got along or agreed on anything, yet here they were, telling me this insane story together.

"And where do you two fit into all of this? Because that's what I want to know."

Asher and Cain looked at each other again.

"Remember how I said angels and demons are the ones who look after and control the souls for the leaders and councils?" Asher asked.

I nodded. "Yeah."

Asher hesitated, and Cain snorted.

"For *Heaven's* sake, Asher, just spit it out." Cain looked over at me. "Asher is an angel, and I'm a demon. We're on opposite teams. Asher is the innocent, pure brother while I'm the big, bad demon brother every mother warns her daughter against. We were both sent to Earth to do the same job."

"And what job is that?" I asked.

"We can't tell you that—not yet," Asher said.

I glared at Asher, but he ignored me.

"I'm sorry, but we can't."

I glared at both of them for a while before finally giving up. Apparently, my glare was as terrifying as a baby kitten. Then, I did something strange. I laughed, and then I laughed some more. "Are you two kidding me? Do you really expect me to believe that I'm sitting in this house with an angel and a demon? Really?"

"I know it sounds crazy, but it is the truth. You wanted to know what we are, so we're telling you." Asher said.

"You are both insane," I said, growing serious.

I stared at the brothers and noticed the intensity in their eyes. They believed every word that they'd said.

"Oh my God, you both really are insane," I said.

Cain growled, "Think about it, Ella. You *know* something's not right with us. That's why you demanded answers. Tell me I'm wrong."

I hesitated, thinking of all the things I'd noticed about the brothers. I knew they were *something*, but an angel and a demon?

"This is a joke," I said finally, refusing to believe they were telling the truth.

"Why would we lie to you?" Asher asked.

"Because you're crazy!" I shouted. "If you're an angel and you're a demon, prove it! You said they have special powers. Well, show me!"

Cain shrugged before standing. "If that's what it takes…"

He disappeared, literally disappeared, right in front of me. I screamed and threw myself back against the couch, willing myself to become one with the cushion. My mind couldn't process what I'd just seen. I looked at the chair, waiting for Cain to reappear so that I'd know I'd just imagined him disappearing into thin air.

"I'm behind you."

I screamed again as I leaped off the couch and spun around. Sure enough, Cain was standing behind the couch. I looked back and forth between him and Asher, unable to process what I had seen.

"What just happened?" I managed to gasp out.

"I can move faster than your eye can follow. Also"—he walked over to the chair—"we have strength that no normal soul possesses."

I watched in horror as he lifted the chair like it weighed nothing. My mouth opened and closed, but no words formed.

"Shit. She's going into shock," Cain said as he put the chair back where it belonged. He rushed to my side and gently pushed me down onto the couch. "Look at me, Ella. I know it's a lot to take in, but we're telling you the truth. You just saw it with your own eyes."

I couldn't take my eyes off of him. "Oh my God, I kissed a demon!"

He chuckled. "And you liked it."

My eyes swung to Asher. He was suddenly looking anywhere but at me.

"She kissed you?" Asher asked Cain.

"You seem surprised, brother."

Asher looked away from both of us. "It doesn't matter. What's important is that you accept all of this, Ella."

"Why? I don't understand any of this. Why do I have to accept it? Why can't I just go back to twenty minutes ago when I thought you two were on drugs or something?" I whispered.

"Because you're in danger," Cain said.

"What?"

"That cloaked figure in your bedroom last night? That was the same figure who turned your kitchen into an icebox."

"Who is he or it or whatever I'm supposed to call the cloaked...thing?"

Asher finally looked at me again. His expression was grave. "You're being stalked by Death, Ella."

"Excuse me?" I asked.

"That cloaked figure is Death. He's the real deal. You're probably the only living person who has actually seen Death and survived to tell the tale."

"But why is he stalking me? I didn't do anything!" I shouted. "And where does he fit in with all of this?"

Cain and Asher looked at each other. I saw Asher shake his head just barely.

"That's what we're going to find out. Until we do, you're in danger. Death doesn't make it a habit to randomly stalk mortals," Asher said.

"And as for where he fits, he doesn't. Death is his own entity. He doesn't choose sides between Heaven and Hell. He simply comes when it's time for a person to die. He takes the life force and releases it. Then, it's up to the angels and demons to decide where that person's soul goes."

"This can't be happening to me." I tried to process what the brothers were saying.

"It is happening. Do you think it's a coincidence that your own mother tried to kill you and you now have Death on your heels? Something big is in play here, and you're right at the center of it all." Cain said, not bothering to sugarcoat the truth.

"So, I'm your job, aren't I?" I asked.

"What?" Asher asked sharply.

"That's why you were both sent here—to watch over me and find out what's really going on. Heaven and Hell are both curious about me."

I couldn't believe that I was taking all of this seriously. If I had any common sense at all, I'd walk out of this house and never look back.

I couldn't though. Just the thought of Death watching me, standing in my kitchen, *my bedroom*, made me want to pee myself.

"They are. I won't lie, but they're not what's important right now. We need to focus on keeping you alive long enough to handle this," Cain said.

I gave him a look of disbelief. "I can't run from Death, Cain. If he's after me, then I'm going to die."

"You're mortal. Of course, you're going to die. *But* it doesn't have to be right now. Although you can't do anything to protect yourself from Death, we can. One of us can hold him off for a while. Together, we can push him away."

Asher looked as if he wanted to speak, but he caught himself at the last moment.

"So, basically, I'm going to have one of you around me at all times." I groaned. "That's just wonderful. I'm being stalked by Death, and a demon and an angel are now my babysitters."

Cain smirked. "It could be worse. I mean, your babysitters could be ugly. Consider yourself lucky. You get to look at one of us at all times."

I flipped him off. He only laughed.

I rested my head in my hands as I tried to process everything I'd just learned. Heaven and Hell were real even if they weren't exactly how they were portrayed in the Bible. Angels and demons existed. They walked among us, harvesting souls to take them back to Heaven and Hell. Souls were at war.

"And to think, I was worried about college a week ago," I mumbled.

I jumped when I felt a hand rest on my shoulder. I looked up to see Asher standing next to me.

"It'll all work out in the end, Ella. I promise." His face was so sincere that I wanted to believe him.

I glanced over at Cain who was curiously watching Asher.

"I do have a question. Actually, I have two," I said.

"What?" Asher asked. "I'll answer them if I can."

"If you're an angel and a demon, don't you two, like, hate each other? You're technically on opposite sides."

Cain chuckled. "That seems to be the story of our lives—and afterlives."

"Being around each other is...hard," Asher answered. "But we both agree that it will take two of us to protect you. We've agreed to work together for now."

I shook my head. "No wonder you two hate each other so much. It's been ingrained in your heads to despise the other."

"What was your other question?" Cain's tone was sharp. Clearly, he was just about finished with this subject.

"Oh, yeah. So, on that paper, it lists the casualties by Loyalists and Patriots. You two are on different lists. How did that happen?"

Cain's entire posture stiffened. "That's a story for a different day."

Then, he disappeared.

Fourteen

"Where have you been?" Uncle Jack demanded as soon as I walked through the front door.

I froze, and Asher, who was walking behind me, bumped into me. Uncle Jack noticed Asher behind me and frowned.

"I, uh…I went over to Asher's house to see if he wanted to help me with some of my homework," I lied.

"And that took you two hours?" He glanced at my empty hands. "Where are your books?"

I glanced behind me and gave Asher a pleading look.

"She had a little bit of trouble waking me up, so she stayed downstairs with my mom until I finally managed to crawl out of bed," Asher lied smoothly as he moved past me and stopped only a few feet away from my uncle.

Uncle Jack still looked skeptical. "Next time you decide to leave the house before I'm even awake, at least leave a note."

"I will. I promise," I said, feeling guilty that I had worried him. I'd been so determined to find out the truth that I hadn't thought my plan through. Obviously, my uncle would have been worried about me after what had happened this weekend with my mother. *If he only knew.*

"Good." He glanced over at Asher. "So, you're one of our new neighbors."

Asher nodded. "Yes, sir. We just moved in last week. Ella has been showing us around. I'm glad that we have such a nice neighbor." He stepped closer to Uncle Jack and rested his hand on my uncle's arm.

"What are you—" Uncle Jack started but stopped speaking mid-sentence.

"Ella is going to be spending a lot of time alone with my brother and me for a while. You're going to let her with no questions asked," Asher said firmly as he stared up at my uncle.

My eyes widened when I saw Asher's eyes glowing just like Cain's had on more than one occasion.

Uncle Jack stared at him, dumbfounded, before nodding. "You and your brother are going to spend time alone with Ella. I won't ask questions." His voice sounded dead.

I shivered.

The room filled with silence as Asher released Uncle Jack and stepped back. After a moment, my uncle shook his head to clear it.

He smiled at both of us. "Well, I won't keep you kids any longer. I'm sure you have a lot of homework to do."

With my mouth hanging open, I watched as my uncle turned and walked into the kitchen, unable to believe what I was seeing.

"Are you coming?" Asher asked.

I looked up to see Asher standing on the bottom step of the staircase. I pressed my lips together as I forced my feet to work. I had several questions, but I wouldn't dare ask them here. If my uncle heard, I would have a lot of explaining to do.

Asher and I made our way up the stairs and down the hallway to my room, both of us silent.

The moment we walked into my room, I closed the door and turned to him. "What was that?" I demanded.

He gave me an innocent look. "What?"

"Don't *what* me! What did you do to my uncle?"

He grinned as he sat down on my bed. "I made sure that he wouldn't cause us any problems in the future. Do you really think he would let us be around you twenty-four/seven if I hadn't…asked him nicely?"

"You…you brainwashed him!" I said.

He shook his head. "No, I just persuaded him."

"You did more than that!" I hesitated. "What did you do?"

He sighed. "I have the ability to persuade mortals if I need to." He held up his hands when he saw the worried expression on my face. "Don't worry. He won't remember what I did, and it won't affect him in any other way."

"How?" I asked stupidly.

He shrugged. "It's one of our gifts. Normally, we don't have to deal with mortals very much, but when we do, it's a nice little trick to have. It makes things a lot easier."

"Is there anything you can't do?" I mumbled.

175

He chuckled. "Yeah, there are a lot of things I'm not capable of."

I walked across the room and sat down on the bed, careful to keep plenty of space between us.

"So, what happens now?" I asked.

After Cain's abrupt departure, I'd been too freaked to ask anything else. Instead, Asher had decided it was time for me to come home before Uncle Jack decided to search for me. Now, I couldn't help but wonder if Asher had somehow known that my uncle was already starting to worry.

"Now, we wait. And we make sure you're protected."

"So, you're basically my bodyguard...my undead bodyguard." I tried to sound playful, but I couldn't quite manage it.

He frowned. "I'm not a zombie, Ella."

"Right, I almost forgot. You're an angel." I sounded insane just saying those words.

He sighed as he lay back on my bed. "Why don't you ask me a few questions before we actually start working on your homework? I'm sure you have a few."

I snorted. "More than a few, but I don't even know where to start."

He stayed silent as I tried to work out exactly what I wanted to ask.

"What kind of abilities do you have—besides what I've seen and what you guys told me earlier?"

He smiled. "I don't want to give away everything about myself, now do I? What you've seen and heard are the main abilities."

"You two sure like to keep secrets, don't you?"

He raised his arms above his head and stretched like a cat. My eyes fell to the tiny slice of skin I could see when his shirt rose. Embarrassed, I quickly looked away.

"After two hundred years, it's easier to just keep the secrets, Ella. It's what we're used to."

I chuckled. "I'm sitting next to an angel who is over two-hundred-years-old. Man, I thought life was difficult before."

"You have no idea just how hard life can be." He seemed to be speaking from experience.

My curiosity got the best of me as I asked my next question, "What happened to you?"

"What do you mean?"

I played with a string on my jeans. "You know, when you…well, died."

When he didn't answer, I chanced a look back at him. He seemed lost in thought, his expression a thousand miles away. Or maybe he was two hundred years away.

"You know that I died in the Battle of Oriskany back in 1777."

I nodded.

"Things were different back then. The colonies were being ripped apart by not only the British, but also from the divide within each. Some wanted a new country where the British could no longer control us. Others, like my parents, were fine with the way things were. They didn't want a war where so many would die. Cain was determined to fight with the Patriots. The moment he signed up for the army, my father kicked him out."

"That's horrible," I whispered.

Asher nodded. "It was. Luckily, one of the other militiamen took him in. Otherwise, he would have been homeless."

"What about you?" I asked.

He glanced at me. "What do you mean?"

"You said your parents were against the war and that Cain joined the Patriots. How did you end up fighting for the Loyalists?"

"Why would you care?" he asked. There was an edge to his voice that I wasn't used to.

"Maybe I like history. Plus, I'd like to know more about you. It's not every day that someone gets to meet an angel."

He studied me for a moment. "Most people hope to never meet an angel or demon until they're very, *very* old." He paused. "As for how I ended up on the opposite side, when it came time for the true war to start, my father finally gave in and joined the Loyalists. I was expected to do the same."

"Even though that put the two of you against Cain?" I asked.

He nodded. "My father exiled him from our family. I don't think it mattered to him."

"What about you?" My voice was soft. "Did it matter to you?"

"I did what I was supposed to do. I listened to my father. Cain seemed to always do the opposite. In a way, it didn't surprise me that we ended up on opposite sides of that war and this one. Everything we've done has always been opposite of each other." He sounded defeated and maybe even sad over that.

"I guess that's how you two ended up on different sides after you died," I said.

"Heaven came to me. Hell went for him. It was pretty cut-and-dry for both of us." He hesitated for a moment. "We were close enough that I watched him choose to go against me. He *knew* that I'd agreed to go to Heaven. The angel who found me said that Heaven would take him, too, but he never gave it the chance. As soon as Hell knocked on his doorstep, he agreed."

"I'm sorry, Asher. Obviously, I could tell there was something going on between you two, but I figured it was just normal brother stuff. I had no idea…" I trailed off.

"Our differences go back further than you could imagine."

"I…I don't know what to say," I told him honestly.

He sat up. "There's nothing you can say. It is what it is."

"But…" I hesitated. "You guys said that Heaven and Hell are at war. Doesn't that mean that you two are still fighting against each other?"

"It does. The only thing I can hope for is that whenever this war is over, we're both still standing. Maybe then we'll be able to put aside our differences and finally come to some sort of truce."

"That's so sad."

He chuckled. "Lots of things in life are sad. Even more are unfair." He looked at me with what I thought was pity. "But you just have to keep moving forward, no matter what fate has in store for you."

"Can I ask you something else?"

"Sure, but I can't promise that I will answer."

I had to give him credit for being honest at least.

"What's it like to die?"

My question seemed to surprise him.

He hesitated for a moment before answering, "Dying was...painful. At least, mine was. It was also terrifying. I was seventeen years old and in the middle of one of the bloodiest battles of the war. I watched my friends, my neighbors, and complete strangers die right before my eyes."

"I can't even imagine," I said quietly. And I couldn't. Reading about battles from the past was one thing, but to actually be there and see the things Asher had seen...I couldn't even begin to comprehend what he'd seen and felt.

"I didn't think it could get any worse until"—he swallowed roughly—"I was hit. The pain was indescribable. The only comfort was that it lasted for just a few seconds. The guns they used back then didn't take bullets like today's. Instead, they used round lead balls. They left quite a...hole in whatever they hit."

I shuddered. "I'm so sorry, Asher. I shouldn't have asked."

He smiled. "No, it's okay. I came to terms with being dead a long time ago. Besides, it's not like I just disappeared from existence. I'm truly home now."

"Are you happy in Heaven? What is it like there?"

His expression softened. "I am happy. It's where I belong. I feel peace there, even when the conflict erupts between us and Hell. I know I'm doing the right thing and protecting those I serve." He paused. "As for what it's like, you'll find out one day, I'm sure. I don't want to ruin it for you, but like I said earlier, it's similar to Earth."

"That's...kind of comforting," I said.

He laughed.

The room filled with silence. It wasn't uneasy though. After everything I'd learned, it was nice to just take a moment to breathe. After a while, Asher moved closer to me. I was surprised when I realized that I had no desire to move away from him.

I gave him a questioning look as he lifted a hand and carefully moved my hair away from my neck.

"I meant to ask earlier, what happened here?" His fingers brushed against the bruises on my neck.

"I went looking for answers. It seems that I only found more questions." I paused. "And a little more trouble."

"What do you mean?" he asked.

"I heard Cain and you talking about my mother that day in my kitchen. I thought maybe she would be able to tell me what I needed to know, so I went to see her."

His eyes found mine. "And did you learn anything from her?"

I shook my head. "She said the same thing as last time. I was supposed to die. She did mention that something must be protecting me." I gave him a skeptical look. "At least she was right about that.

You and your brother have been watching out for me. I can't help but wonder how she knew that."

He shrugged. "Some mortals are more in touch with the other realms. She could very well be one of them. That would explain why she used to drink so much."

He ran his fingers over my bruises again. I shivered at his soft touch.

"I assume she's the reason you have those bruises now."

"Who else would have tried to strangle me? Of course these are from her. The woman just can't seem to keep her hands off of me when I'm within five feet of her."

"I'm sorry she hurt you—again."

I tried to keep the pain I was feeling out of my expression. "With her, it's what I expect. She did tell me she loved me and she even looked as if she felt bad this time. I guess that's something."

He sighed as he finally moved his hand away from me. I squeaked in surprise when he suddenly pulled me to him and hugged me.

"Life is so very unfair. It seems you've had to deal with more than most. For that, I'm sorry."

Unsure of what to do, I hesitantly hugged him back. "It's okay. You and Cain will keep me safe for now, and once all of this is over, I'll leave here and find some peaceful existence where I'm just a normal girl."

Asher's body tensed for a moment before relaxing again. "I'm so sorry."

I finally pulled away when I started to feel uncomfortable. "Hey, it's fine. I'll deal. I always do."

He seemed bothered by my words. I rested my hand on his shoulder, hoping to give him some kind of comfort. He looked down to where my hand rested, seeming surprised that I would so willingly touch him.

"Asher, what's wrong?"

"Nothing. Just lost in thought I suppose." He reached up and rested his hand on top of mine. "I'm surprised you'd want to touch me after all you've learned."

I hesitated for a moment, trying to think of the right way to describe how I felt. "I was freaked. Hell, I'm still freaked. I mean, come on, if our roles were reversed, you'd react the same way."

He chuckled. "Ella, if there were two of you in this world, I wouldn't be freaked. I'd be in Heaven."

I felt my cheeks warm, but I ignored him as I continued, "Even though I'm kind of freaking out, I still like you. I haven't a clue why, but I do. You're a good...person, Asher. Anyone who spends any time with you at all would know that. Being an angel doesn't change that about you."

He gave me a tiny smile. "You're something special, Ella Wilkins. I hope you know that."

Our eyes locked again, and I felt myself getting pulled in. Asher lowered his head just a fraction of an inch, and I realized I had moved closer, too. Our faces were only a few inches apart. My heart started thundering in my chest when I realized that I wanted to kiss the boy next to me. That was wrong on so many levels. He was an angel. That right there should have been reason enough. Add in the fact that I'd kissed his brother, and it was enough for me to abruptly pull away.

I saw disappointment flash across his face, but it was gone in an instant. I wondered if I'd imagined it.

Asher cleared his throat. "Anyway, we really do have homework that needs to get finished. Why don't we get started on it?"

I grinned. "What? The angel can't just magically make his homework do itself?"

"Sadly, no. Trust me, I tried—several times," he teased.

I stood and walked across the room to where my backpack was. "Let's get started then."

And that was how I ended up working on my homework with an angel. My life was officially insane.

Fifteen

When Cain walked through my bedroom door later that night, Asher quickly said good-bye to me before practically running out of the room.

Asher had been extremely quite while we worked on our homework and throughout the rest of the day. I was sure that he was thinking about his past and all the things I'd forced him to remember. Guilt gnawed at my insides. I'd hurt Asher without even meaning to.

"So, do you want me to lift more furniture? Or have we moved past the denial stage?" Cain asked once Asher was gone.

"You can leave my furniture where it is. Thanks," I said in greeting.

Cain smirked, obviously over his little fit from that morning. "Now, you know our dirty little secret."

"I suppose I do," I said.

"Aren't you going to start asking me questions? Or maybe you'll gush like a schoolgirl over how awesome I am." He paused. "Oh, wait. You *are* a schoolgirl. Gush away."

I rolled my eyes. "You're ridiculous."

"Yet you still find me charming enough to kiss—twice. I must be doing something right." He dropped down onto my bed.

"Please, make yourself at home," I said sarcastically. "And we're not talking about that—ever."

"Why not?" he asked.

I hated the fact that he was still smirking at me.

"Because I said so. That's a good enough reason."

He opened his mouth, but I held up my hand.

"Enough, demon. If you're going to stay with me all night, then don't talk. It'll make things so much easier."

He mocked me by pretending to zip his lips shut. Tonight was going to drag on forever. I was sure of it.

An hour later, I lay on my stomach in bed, trying to read a book—emphasis on the word *trying*. It was rather distracting to have Cain sitting against the far wall, constantly moving or humming. Every time I looked up, he would be staring at me.

"Will you look somewhere else?" I finally said when I couldn't take his staring any longer.

"Can't. You never know when Death might sneak back into your room. I don't want to take my eyes off of you for a second."

I groaned. "So, you're going to follow me into the bathroom, too?"

He smirked. "I can if you'd like. I can even help you out while you shower."

"Um, no. I think I'll pass," I said.

He shrugged. "Your loss. I guess I'll just stand outside the door while you do whatever it is girls do when they spend an hour in the bathroom."

"You haven't been alive since 1777. I'm pretty sure they didn't have indoor plumbing back then. So, how do you know how long a girl spends in the bathroom?" I shot back.

His smirk turned into a full-out grin. "I come to Earth a lot to collect souls. Sometimes, I have downtime. I find ways to entertain myself."

I groaned. "You're gross. I can't believe you actually follow girls into the bathroom."

"Hey, even I have morals. If they start getting naked, I leave."

"What a gentleman," I mumbled as I turned my attention back to my book.

I made it through all of two pages before he spoke again, "I'm bored."

"Go watch some girls," I said, not bothering to take my eyes off of my book.

"I'm watching one now. Still bored."

I finally glanced up. "What do you expect me to do about it?"

"Let's go somewhere."

I looked up at the clock. "It's ten thirty. There's nothing open this late. Plus, we have school tomorrow."

"Who cares about school?"

"I do. You've already found your permanent job placement. I, on the other hand, need to graduate, so I can go out into the big, bad world in a few months. I doubt I'll make it far if I lack a high school diploma," I said, not bothering to hide my sarcasm.

"You're so boring. If I hadn't already died, I would have died of boredom within the first five minutes of babysitting you," he grumbled.

"You know, for a demon, you're kind of whiny."

He rolled his eyes. "This demon needs to stretch his legs. Come on."

"No," I said stubbornly.

He was silent for a minute. "I'm sure you're curious about what I do as a demon."

"Not really," I lied.

"Liar."

I finally gave up on reading. I closed my book and tossed it on the floor. "Fine, great demon master, tell me all about your job. Does it have benefits? How long until you can retire? Do they let you take vacations?"

He stood. "Someone took their sarcastic pill tonight, didn't they?"

"I can't help it. You bring out the worst parts of me."

He walked across the room and held out his hand. "Come with me. I'll *show* you what a demon does. It'll be fun." He grinned. "Plus, it'll be a learning experience. I know you're all about the learning."

I groaned. "You're impossible."

Still, my curiosity was piqued. I wanted to know what exactly Mr. Demon planned to show me. I reached up and grabbed his hand to pull myself up. Instead, my entire body locked up. I literally froze in place. Before I could blink, everything went black. I felt wind rushing past me, blowing strands of my hair away from my face.

As soon as it started, it was over. I gasped for breath and held on to Cain's hand for dear life as I tried to recover.

"See? That wasn't so bad, was it?" he asked.

I looked up. We were no longer in my bedroom. Instead, we were standing in a narrow alleyway. Tall brick buildings surrounded us. I could hear a car horn honking off in the distance.

"What…what did you do?" My entire body shook as I clung to Cain's hand.

"I transported us to a more entertaining location." He grinned. "Welcome to London, Ella."

I gaped at him. "London?"

He nodded. "Traveling with me is so much faster than flying, don't you think? Plus, it's free."

"I…I don't understand. We're on a different *continent!*"

"I see you paid attention in geography class."

He patted me on the head. I slapped his hand away.

"I can travel—fast. It's one of my abilities."

"What are we doing here?" I tried not to think about the fact that I'd traveled across an ocean in only a second.

"Working. Come on." He started walking.

When I didn't move, he tugged until my feet finally got the message. He kept my hand in his as we moved out of the alley and down a street. There wasn't another soul around. I expected him to keep to the shadows just to be safe, but he strolled right down the street like it wasn't the middle of the night, and he wasn't a demon.

"Shouldn't you be stealthier or something?" I whispered.

He laughed loudly. "I can shield myself, Ella. I'm shielding you, too."

"Shielding?" I asked stupidly.

"If anyone were to walk by us right now, they'd never see us. We're invisible."

"Oh," I said. "Wait a minute. I know you can do that to yourself, but how am I invisible, too?"

He squeezed my hand. "As long as I touch you, you're shielded."

"Well, that's a nifty little trick," I said as we walked past a black car with heavily tinted windows.

"Indeed it is. Now, hurry up, or we'll be late."

He quickened his pace, forcing me to do the same. A few blocks over, he stopped abruptly.

"Hey," I grumbled. "What are you doing?"

He held his finger up to his lips. "Shh."

I rolled my eyes. "You just said no one can see or hear us. Why do I have to be quiet now?"

"Because"—he pointed up at the building in front of us—"Death is here."

Pure unadulterated fear coursed through my body. I took a step back, but Cain tightly held on to my hand.

"Why did you bring me here if *he's* here?" I asked frantically.

"Calm down, Ella. He's not here for you."

"Then, who—" I stopped midsentence when I noticed two figures dressed entirely in black carefully making their way down the fire escape on the side of the building.

Once they reached the ground, they glanced around, looking right through us, before slipping into the shadows and out of sight.

"Who was that?" I asked.

"Doesn't matter. They're not who we're here for."

Before I could say anything else, the world went black, and the wind rushed past me again. Then, we were standing in the middle of a living room.

"Now, where are we?" I asked.

"Top floor. Death has been here. Now, it's my turn," Cain answered. When I opened my mouth to speak, he shook his head. "Just watch."

He stared down a long hallway. After a few seconds, I started to grow impatient, wondering if he was just messing with me.

Finally, something happened. One minute, the hallway was pitch-black. The next, a blinding light was in its place. I shielded my eyes with my free hand as they started to water from the intensity.

"Ella, I have to let go of your hand now," Cain said.

"What? Why?" I asked.

"Because I have a job to do."

Before I could protest, he released me. Instantly, the bright light disappeared, as did Cain. Fearing that he'd left me behind, I spun in a circle, searching the room for him, but I found nothing.

"Cain?" I whispered. When he didn't answer, I called his name again, louder this time, but still nothing.

"Don't panic," I said. Then, I laughed. "Sure, don't panic. I'm only an ocean away from home. No reason to panic at all. I'll just find the nearest police station and ask them to fly me home."

As if I wasn't freaked enough, another thought occurred to me. Cain had said Death was here right before he had done his little magic act to bring us to this room. Maybe he didn't want to protect me after all. Maybe he wanted to deliver me to Death himself.

Fear clawed at my insides, shredding them. If that were his plan, I was already dead.

No. He wouldn't do that, I told myself.

Cain was sarcastic and even a little perverted at times, but he wasn't evil. He wouldn't do that to me. Plus, if Death were nearby, this room would be a freezer by now.

I looked around again, expecting Death to be watching me. The room remained empty. I turned my attention back to the hallway where the light had been. Maybe Cain was back there, hiding.

I crept carefully down the hallway. When I reached the end, there was a single door. I raised my hand to push it open. As soon as my fingers touched the wood, a hand touched my shoulder. Already spooked, I let out a shrill scream.

"Shut up!" Cain hissed as he clamped a hand over my mouth.

I whimpered into it.

"I'm going to let you go. Don't scream, okay?"

I nodded, and he released me. I instantly spun around to face him.

"Where did you go?" I demanded.

"I had to take the souls to Hell," he said.

I blinked. "Excuse me?"

"Those bright lights you saw? Those were souls. I had to lead them to Hell."

"Oh." I still didn't understand. "But they disappeared as soon as you did."

"Because I let go of you. Once the connection was broken, you couldn't see what was happening. Souls are only visible to Death, angels, and demons. You're mortal."

"So, you never really left then. I just couldn't see you."

"Bingo."

I fought the urge to hit him. To distract myself, I turned back toward the door. "What's in here?" I stepped closer to the door and raised my hand to open it.

"*Ella.*" Cain's voice was sharp. "Don't open that door."

"Why?" I asked, taken aback by his harsh tone.

"Because the two souls I took to Hell left behind bodies. They're in that room."

I swallowed. "Oh."

"Yeah, and let's just say their deaths weren't exactly natural."

"Those two people we saw earlier…they were here, weren't they? They killed the people behind this door."

"I think you've seen enough. Let's go."

He grabbed my hand. Once again, everything went black, and wind blew past my face. When I opened my eyes, we were back in my room, standing beside my bed.

I let go of Cain and sat down. He stood in front of me, watching me.

I finally managed to get out the words, "That was…different."

"It was so much better than sitting here, watching you read a book," Cain said. His whole body seemed to relax once he realized I wasn't going to freak out.

"Next time you decide to take me on a field trip, let me know, okay?" I asked.

"What's the fun in that?"

"Cain," I warned.

"Fine." He sighed. "Why don't you try to get some sleep?"

"That's the best idea you've had all night," I grumbled. I stood and pulled the covers back. I ignored Cain as I climbed into bed and shut the light off on my nightstand.

"Where are you going to sleep?" I asked once I was settled in.

"I planned on sleeping on the floor, but if you're game, I'll join you in bed."

"Here's an idea. Why don't you go sleep in *your* bed? It's like fifteen feet away. I'm sure you can babysit me from there."

"No can do, sunshine," he said cheerfully.

"Fine. Enjoy the floor." I rolled away from him, hoping that he'd take the hint and leave me alone.

It seemed that he did. Cain didn't say another word as I slowly drifted off to sleep, secretly comforted that he was watching over me.

That night, my dreams were filled with shadowy figures dressed in black and brilliant white light.

Sixteen

"Wake up, princess, or you're going to be late."

I groaned as I pulled my covers over my head, hoping that Cain would go away, but I had no such luck. The covers were ripped off of me. I peeled my eyes open to see Cain standing above me, smirking. His hair was wet, and he had changed his clothes. Obviously, he'd felt secure enough to shower and leave me alone.

"I thought you weren't going to let me out of your sight," I pointed out.

"Don't worry. Asher watched over you while I made myself pretty. Now, get up. We're going to be late, and I know you can't have that."

"If I have to wake up to your smiling face every morning from now on, I'll probably off myself before Death has the chance," I grumbled as I climbed out of bed.

"Like I'd let you do that." He sat down on my bed and watched me pull clothes out of my drawers and closet.

I grabbed a scarf off the top shelf of my closet to hide the bruises around my neck.

"I'm going to go shower now. If I catch you in my bathroom, I'll stab you with my toothbrush," I said as I walked across the room to the door.

"Like you'd be able to see me," he called after me.

I ignored him as I left the room and headed to the bathroom. I tossed my clothes on the counter and turned on the hot water. After it warmed up, I climbed inside and sighed. I already felt better, and it wasn't just the water. This was the first moment of peace I'd had since I stormed over to the brothers' house yesterday.

I'd spent the last six months alone, spending time with only Amanda. I'd become a loner. Now that I was constantly stuck with Cain or Asher, I realized how little I'd missed human interaction.

Not that they're exactly human, but that's beside the point.

I seriously hoped that Cain and Asher figured out why Death was so interested in me. The sooner, the better. I wasn't sure how long I could deal with them constantly hovering over me and annoying me every five seconds.

Whatever was happening, I knew it was big. I wasn't a fool. I knew there was no way Hell and Heaven would send an angel and a demon down to watch over one girl if something major weren't happening. That didn't bode well for me.

I took as long as I dared in the shower, fearing both Cain storming in to check on me and ending up late for school, before climbing out. I toweled off and dressed quickly. I dried my hair before pulling it back into a loose braid. I wrapped the scarf around my neck, careful to make sure it covered all the bruises. I didn't spend a lot of time on my makeup. Instead, I only lined my eyes and put on a little bit of lip gloss. I didn't have time for anything else.

When I opened the bathroom door, I jumped back. Cain was standing right outside the door.

No, it wasn't Cain. *Asher.*

Cain was wearing a black shirt, and the boy in front of me was wearing light blue.

"I swear, I'm going to get you two name tags, Asher," I said as I moved past him and back into my room.

"How did you know it was me?" he asked.

"Your shirt. Cain always wears black. You tend to gravitate toward lighter-colored clothes."

He seemed surprised by my answer. Then, he laughed. "I never noticed that before. You're very observant, Ella."

"I had to figure out a way to tell you two apart. I mean, if Cain speaks, I instantly know it's him. If he keeps his mouth closed, it takes me a second to figure it out."

He shook his head, still grinning. "Are you ready to go?"

I grabbed my backpack off the floor and turned back to him. "Yep, let's go."

I followed him back to the door. I stopped at my calendar and marked another day off.

Asher watched me intently. "What's that for?"

"It's a countdown to my freedom. Graduation—that's when I can escape this place. It makes me happy to mark another day off. It means I'm that much closer to my future."

Asher's hands clenched at his sides, but he didn't say a word. Instead, he turned and left the room.

I shook my head as I followed him. Sometimes, Asher made absolutely no sense.

Asher stuck to me like glue until the first bell rang.

We'd attracted attention from our fellow classmates as soon as we pulled into the parking lot, but I'd forced myself to ignore their stares. Eventually, they would get used to Cain and Asher hanging around me all the time. Until then, I was sure there would be plenty of rumors about us. It was strange to realize that I hadn't cared about what they thought since the first time I walked through the front doors after my mother's attack. My life was far too complicated to worry about any of them.

When the bell did ring, I smugly told Asher good-bye and hurried away. The brothers might be determined to follow me around outside of school, but there was no way they could follow me to classes that we didn't share. That meant I had two periods to myself. I practically skipped to my locker with that thought bouncing around inside my head.

I unloaded my backpack and grabbed what I needed for history. I started to walk down the hall when the hairs on the back of my neck stood on end. I stopped dead, terrified that Death had decided to pay me a visit at school.

Death at school—that's about the worst way to go that I can think of.

I turned around, searching the hallway. My eyes landed on Cain. He was leaning against his locker, watching me. When I realized that he was watching me instead of Death, I relaxed. I flipped him off before hurrying down the hallway in the opposite direction. I was determined to avoid him as much as I could when I had the chance.

Once I sat down in history class, I pulled my homework out of my notebook. I checked over my answers as my classmates slowly made their way to their seats.

"Hey, Ella?" a voice said.

I looked up to see Stacey, the blonde leader of the girls, who sat in front of me.

"Yeah?" I asked cautiously.

Even before my fall from grace, Stacey and I had never talked much. Afterward, we didn't talk at all. Her sudden decision to speak to me had me instantly on guard.

"I was just wondering how you know the Collins twins." She smiled sweetly.

I fought not to groan out loud. Of course, they would be the reason she'd suddenly decided I was worthy of her speaking to me again.

"They live…close to me." I'd almost said they were my neighbors, but I'd decided against it. With my luck, girls would randomly show up on their doorstep, and I'd be the one to blame.

"Oh. I noticed that they seem to hang around you a lot."

I nodded. "Yeah, I suppose. We're friends. Kind of."

"That's cool. You know, you're always welcome to join my friends and me at lunch. I've been meaning to invite you for forever, but I kept forgetting. Plus, Jenny seems to have it out for you. I didn't want to get on her bad side."

It took every fiber of my being not to laugh in her face. Of course, she'd suddenly decided I was worthy of her presence.

"Thanks for the offer, but I wouldn't want you to tick off Jenny on my account."

She laughed. "Jenny isn't a problem anymore. Your two friends made sure of that. You should sit with me today. Bring them with you."

"I'll think about it," I said, knowing there was no way I would go anywhere near her table today or any other day.

"Great!" She smiled as she turned away.

I rolled my eyes.

If she or anyone else thought they could get close to Asher and Cain through me, they were out of their minds. If they had any idea what Cain and Asher really were, they'd run away, screaming. The thought of every female in the surrounding area running from Cain, screaming bloody murder, made me smile. He thought he was so good with the ladies. It would be good to see him knocked down a bit.

"Is this seat taken?"

My head whipped to the side. Asher stood beside the desk to my left, grinning.

"How did you—what are you doing here?" I asked.

"It seems that there was an issue with my schedule. I had to have a few of my classes switched around."

I clenched my pencil so tightly that it snapped. Asher chuckled as he sat down beside me.

"Wonderful," I muttered.

"Isn't it? It's almost like…fate."

I flipped him off just as the teacher walked into the room. She shot me a dirty look, but luckily, she decided not to call me out on it. I slumped down in my seat, defeated.

Stacey turned and gave Asher a smile so big that I worried her face might actually crack in two. He politely smiled back.

"Wonderful," I repeated, mumbling it quietly under my breath.

My escape from Cain and Asher was officially over. It had lasted a wonderful fifteen minutes.

The rest of my morning consisted of Asher following me around. Amanda noticed the way he trailed after me, but all she could do was give me a questioning look since Asher was with us.

At lunchtime, Asher got in line behind us. Amanda's confused look in math class changed to a tiny grin. Her eyes kept darting back and forth between Asher and me. I knew what she thought—that Asher was *with* me.

Even before I'd found out about Death and when the brothers had started sticking to me, she had told me that she thought Asher was into me. With the way he was acting now, I knew there was no way I could deny it without telling her the truth, not that she'd believe me.

As soon as we sat down at our table, Amanda cursed. "I forgot my milk. I'll be right back."

I waited until she was far enough away that she couldn't hear us before turning to Asher. "We need to talk."

"About what?" he asked.

"Us. And Amanda. She's not stupid, Asher. She has already noticed how you're constantly hanging around me. What am I supposed to tell her?"

"Anything but the truth," Asher said seriously. "She can't know what is really happening."

"No shit, Sherlock," I growled. "I know she can't know what's really going on. I just don't know what to tell her."

He tapped his fingers on the table for a moment before speaking, "Tell her we're together."

I nearly choked on my food. "Excuse me?"

He shrugged. "She already suspects that we are. Plus, it's the most believable explanation."

"How do you know that?" I demanded, worried that he had been listening in on my conversations with her.

He gave me a look that said he questioned my intelligence. "She isn't exactly hard to read. Besides, she's not the only one wondering whether we're together or not."

"Why can't she say she's with me? That'd be way more believable," Cain said as he sat down at the table.

"Oh, goodie. I'm stuck with both of you at once. Just when I thought things couldn't get worse," I said in greeting.

"Things can always get worse. It's the way of the world," Cain said as he picked up a fry.

"I'm with her more than you are, Cain. It would make more sense if she said she was with me," Asher said, looking at Cain.

He shrugged. "Whatever makes you happy, dear brother. But don't pretend that it's just for show. That'd be an insult to Ella's intellect."

"What are you talking about?" Asher asked.

Cain chuckled. "Oh, don't act so innocent. We both know you'd love to—" He stopped talking as Amanda slid back into her seat.

"Hey, Cain," she said, oblivious to the tension around her.

I looked back and forth between the two brothers, trying to understand what was going on. They were openly glaring at each other. I was surprised that Asher looked even angrier than Cain. They had told me that they planned to work together to protect me. Looking at them now, I had to assume that I would be on my own if Death suddenly decided to join us for lunch since the brothers would be too busy killing each other to notice.

"So…" Amanda said, finally catching on to the tension surrounding us. "How was your weekend, Ella?"

"It was kind of boring," I said, not daring to glance at Cain or Asher. "Just the usual."

"Oh, don't be modest, Ella," Cain said loudly.

Amanda looked at him. "What do you mean?"

"Asher and Ella spent the whole weekend together—*alone*." Cain innocently smiled at me, which made me want to reach across the table and smack him.

"Cain…" Asher warned.

"Oh, come on, Asher. There's no need to be shy. The whole world should know that you and Ella are together." His voice was loud enough that it carried to the tables around us.

I glanced around to see several students watching me. Most of the girls had a look of disbelief on their faces.

"What are you playing at?" I demanded.

"Nothing." He was still grinning.

Around me, I could hear people whispering my name along with Asher's. By the end of lunch, everyone would be talking about my new *relationship* with Asher. I wanted to crawl under the table and hide.

I glanced at Amanda. She was watching me with a frown on her face.

"Why didn't you tell me?" she asked quietly.

"We didn't want anyone to know, Amanda," Asher said. "This is brand-new, and we wanted to see if it would work out or not before we decided to announce it to anyone."

Amanda was hurt. I could tell by the look on her face. I instantly felt guilty even though I had no reason to. Cain was the one who deserved the guilt.

"You could've at least told me. I'm your best friend." Amanda stood. "I need to go to the library before class. I'll see you later."

I watched as she quickly walked away. She was hurt and angry. I understood why, but there was no way I could tell her the truth about what was really going on. I'd rather her be angry with me than put her in danger.

"Was it something I said?" Cain asked with a smirk.

Amanda spent the rest of the day avoiding me. It wasn't hard to do since the only afternoon class we shared was gym. Still, she went out of her way to stay away from me in the locker room. We played volleyball in gym, and we were placed on opposite teams, giving her the perfect excuse to keep from speaking to me.

I felt awful. Amanda was the only real friend I had, and she thought I had been keeping things from her. I'd never done that to her before. No, we didn't speak about my mother, but I'd told her everything else. I knew she saw my silence as a betrayal, but there was nothing I could do to set her straight.

Cain, on the other hand, would be getting an earful as soon as we were out of school. From the way he was smirking, I had no doubt that he would enjoy it.

Jerk.

I had no idea why he had lied, but I was sure it was benefiting him in some way.

Asher stuck close to me, but we didn't speak. He seemed just as angry with his brother's lie as I was. Maybe that was Cain's plan all along. It seemed he did things just to drive Asher mad. It definitely seemed to be working this time.

I couldn't understand why Cain pushed Asher the way he did. Obviously, they had a messy history. I had known that before Asher told me just how far back their divide went. Still, they were brothers. If I had a sibling, I would try everything to ensure that we remained at least civil toward each other. I thought Asher would have, too, if it wasn't for Cain constantly trying to get under his skin. Cain seemed to relish in Asher's anger though.

Cain and I ignored each other in our afternoon class together, except for when the bell rang. He grabbed my arm to keep me from leaving my seat.

"What?" My tone was nasty.

If he noticed, he didn't let on.

"Tell Asher to bring you to our house this afternoon when you get home. Wear something comfortable."

"Why?" I demanded.

"You'll see." With that, he released me and stood.

I watched as he slowly strolled out of the room, as if he didn't have a care in the world.

I grumbled as I followed him out of the room and down the hallway to our lockers. He glanced back a couple of times, probably to make sure Death wasn't creeping down the hallway behind us, intent on grabbing me and shoving me into a janitor's closet to kill me.

Asher was waiting next to my locker when I rounded the corner. Cain walked by him without even a glance in his direction. Asher managed to peel his eyes away from me long enough to shoot Cain a glare. I stopped next to Asher and opened my locker to grab my book for the last class of the day. He stood next to me, remaining silent. I would bet my savings that if he wasn't on guard duty, he would be as far away from me as possible.

Wonderful, I thought to myself as we made our way to my last class.

Cain was the jerk who had started all of this, yet Asher and Amanda were both giving me the silent treatment.

As expected, Asher followed me inside. He'd had his schedule changed since neither brother had been with me in this class. He sat down next to me without a word. All through class, I kept glancing at him, but he never once looked my way. Annoyed, I shot out of my seat as soon as the bell rang, not caring if he could manage to keep up with me or not. I stopped by my locker for my books and bag, ignoring Asher when he stopped next to me.

"Do you need a ride home?" he asked.

"The way you're acting, I think I'll be better off walking." I slammed my locker shut.

"Ella—"

"What?" I stopped and turned to him.

"Look, I'm sorry." He glanced around the hallway. "Can we talk in my car? Please?"

A begging angel—that was a sight to behold.

"Sure, we can talk. But that requires you actually speaking to me. I just want to make sure you realized that." I didn't try to keep the sarcasm out of my tone.

"I'm aware." He rested his hand on my lower back and guided me down the hall to the stairs.

People watched us as we passed by, but I ignored them, too preoccupied with my anger.

When we reached Asher's car, he held the door open, and I climbed in. He shut it behind me before walking around the front and climbing in himself.

Instead of starting the car, he just sat there.

"Are we leaving or not?" I asked after a minute or two.

"We need to talk first," Asher said.

I raised an eyebrow. "Then, by all means, start talking."

He sighed. "I'm sorry for what Cain did this afternoon, Ella."

"Why are you apologizing for him?" I asked.

"Because we both know that he won't. Plus, he never would've said anything if I hadn't suggested that we pretend."

"It's not your fault that he's an ass. But I still don't understand why you've been giving me the silent treatment."

He turned to look at me. "I thought you were angry with me, too."

I rolled my eyes. "You didn't do anything, Asher—well, besides giving me the silent treatment. I thought you were mad at me for some reason."

"I could never be angry with you, Ella." He sighed again. "As usual, Cain has a way of screwing up everything."

"Hey"—I reached over and took his hand—"don't worry about it, okay? I'm not mad at you, and you're not mad at me. Let's focus all our energy on being angry at Cain."

He chuckled. "That, I can do."

"I still don't get why he decided to announce it like that," I said.

Asher started his car and backed out of his parking spot. "He was trying to get to me," he said quietly.

"But why?" I asked.

"It doesn't matter." He shook his head. "Anyway, do you have plans for this evening?"

"No…yes. Cain said to tell you to bring me to your house when we get home. I have no idea why, but I'm supposed to wear something comfortable. I'm betting he wants me to go running with him again or something." I snorted. "Like that's going to happen."

"You should go," Asher said, surprising me.

"What? Why? I thought we were mad at him."

He grinned. "We are, but it'll be good for you."

"Spending a few hours with Cain will be anything but good for me."

"If anyone can handle Cain, it's you. Just don't let him get to you. Show him who's boss."

"Maybe I can accidentally trip him or something." I wasn't even ashamed at how much joy that thought brought me.

"If you do, make sure to get it on video. *Please.*"

"Is it even possible to trip you guys?" I asked seriously. "Aren't angels supposed to be full of grace? I'm sure demons are like cats, always landing on their feet."

Asher looked at me like I was nuts.

"What? I was trying to make a funny."

"I've never really thought about it, but I suppose we could trip. I mean, when we're visible on Earth, we can eat and sleep, so I'm sure we can trip, too."

"So, you don't eat or sleep in Heaven or Hell?"

He shook his head. "Nope. There's no need."

"I suppose not," I said thoughtfully.

I knew what Cain and Asher were, but there were so many things that I *didn't* know. If I let myself dwell on it, I knew I would go mad.

"One more question," I said.

Asher pulled into his driveway. "What?"

"Okay, so people obviously don't always die right in the prime of their lives, right? I mean, most people live to be very old. When they die and you take them to Heaven, do they look like they did when they died or what?"

"In Heaven, most keep the form of their soul. We can choose to take on our human form if we want to though. The soldiers do when we go into battle. We can decide to be any age, but most of the time, we look like we did when we were in our early twenties—you know, the prime of our lives."

"What about…" I swallowed, hating the words that were about to come out of my mouth. "What about kids who died?"

"Their souls, just like all others, are ageless, so when they pass to Heaven or Hell, they're fully matured. If they choose to take on a human form, they can pick any age, just like everyone else."

"That's so weird," I mumbled.

He laughed. "Of all the things you've learned, that's what you think is weird?"

"I'm just trying to picture it—souls walking around like big light bulbs with normal-looking people next to them. It's just strange."

"The rules of this realm don't apply to Heaven and Hell." He paused. "How do you know what a soul looks like?"

"What do you mean?" I asked.

"You said you pictured the souls walking around like big light bulbs. How do you know that's what they look like?"

"Oh," I said, realizing my mistake. "I just guessed?" My lie sounded feeble, even to my own ears.

"Ella," he warned.

"All right, fine. Cain took me out on a job. I saw a soul."

Asher stared at me with his mouth hanging open. "He did *what?*"

"It was no big deal. Honest."

He shook his head. "He shouldn't have shown you that, Ella."

"Why not?" I demanded.

"Because! You're not a part of our world. He had no right."

"So, it's okay for Death to stalk me and for you and Cain to follow me around every moment of every day, but it's not okay for me to see a soul? That makes no sense!"

"I just want you to have a normal life for as long as you can. That's all!"

"Well, guess what? My life hasn't been normal for six months. I don't think it'll go back to normal anytime soon either."

I climbed out of the car before he could say another word. I slammed the door, letting my anger get the best of me. I stormed across his yard to mine and walked up to my front door. I unlocked it and slipped inside before locking it behind me. I knew that it wouldn't keep Asher out, but hopefully, he'd get the message and leave me alone.

I needed *me* time. Even if it was for only a few minutes, I needed it.

For once, luck was with me. Asher didn't come for me.

Seventeen

"Are you going to sit up here all night and pout?" Cain asked as he appeared in the middle of my room.

I didn't even startle. I was starting to get used to the way they could both appear out of thin air.

"Actually, I'm not pouting. I'm pretending that neither of you exist. I find that I'm much happier that way," I shot back.

He walked over to my computer desk where I was trying to work on my homework.

"You don't really mean that. Your life is so much more interesting now that we're in it."

"Go away, Cain. I've been up here by myself for over an hour, and Death hasn't tried to kill me. Take the night off. Find a pretty hooker. Drag a few souls to Hell. Just do something far away from me."

"Oh, you're funny when you're grumpy. I'll have to remember that."

I ignored him as I continued with my homework.

"So…I guess you're angry at me for today, and you're angry at Asher because he's mad at me for taking you out with me to collect souls. That isn't confusing at all. One would think you'd agree with him since you're angry with me."

"That doesn't even make sense," I growled.

"It does to me."

"Why did you do it?"

"Do what?" His tone was far too innocent.

"Embarrass me today by telling everyone that I'm with Asher. You embarrassed him, too, I think. Plus, you made Amanda hate me."

He shrugged. "The mortal will get over it. You and Asher will, too."

I glared at him. "You do anything and everything you can to tick off your brother. Did you ever think that you two might actually get along if you weren't such a—"

He cut me off, "Uh, language, Ella. And even if I weren't…*me*, I would still manage to fight with Asher. It's just the way things are between us."

"It doesn't have to be," I told him. "If you both tried, I think you might actually get along."

"Doubtful. We couldn't get along when we were alive. Why start now?"

I sighed. "You're impossible."

"Did you ever think that maybe I wasn't trying to embarrass both of you today?"

I looked up at him. "Then, what were you trying to do?"

Cain leaned down so that our faces were inches apart. "Maybe I was trying to help him."

"Help him how?"

He chuckled as he pulled away. "It doesn't matter. What *does* matter is that you blew me off this afternoon. No one blows me off and gets away with it. Get changed. We're going to my house."

"You seriously think I'm going anywhere with you?" I asked.

"Oh, I know you are. If you don't, I'll drag you out of here myself. Now, go."

"You wouldn't."

Even I knew that was a lie. Cain was enough of a pain to do just that.

"I think we both know I would. Hurry up before I decide I'm tired of waiting."

I glared at him as I stood. "I'm only going along with this because I know you won't leave me alone."

I ignored his grin as I walked to my dresser and pulled out a loose-fitting shirt and sweatpants. I made my way to the bathroom and changed quickly. After tossing my clothes in the hamper, I opened the door. Cain was standing in the hallway, waiting for me.

"Took you long enough," he said as he started walking.

I sighed as I followed him down the stairs and out the front door. When we walked into his house, I looked around for Asher.

"He's not here," Cain said without turning to look at me. "He left once he finished lecturing me."

"He's all about the lectures these days," I said as I followed him into the kitchen.

I looked around, curious, since I'd never seen their kitchen before. It was as simple as the living room. There were no decorations of any kind. A stove was off to my right with a microwave above it. To my left was the refrigerator. The light-colored wood cabinets were paired with cream countertops.

"Besides the refrigerator, we don't use this room much," Cain said as he opened a door. "We're both too lazy to cook. Plus, neither of us knows how. Ordering takeout is much easier."

Not sure what to say to that, I kept silent. Cain motioned for me to follow him as he started walking down a set of steps. Curious, I followed. The stairs were dimly lit with barely enough light for me to see the steps below my feet. I held on to the rail to keep from falling to my death. When I reached the bottom, Cain was nowhere in sight, swallowed by the darkness.

Feeling uneasy, I felt along the wall for a light switch. I couldn't find one. "Cain?"

I blinked when an overhead light came on. Cain was standing underneath it.

"Yes?"

I shook my head. "Nothing."

I looked around the basement, wondering why he had brought me here. It was empty, except for a locked chest in the far corner.

"Why are we down here?" I asked.

"Because," Cain said as he walked over to the chest, "I want to show you something."

I walked over to him as he opened the chest, curious about what was inside.

"A sword?" I asked, surprised when I saw what it was.

"Two swords actually." He pulled both of them out of the chest.

"Uh…cool?" I said, completely lost.

"I'm glad you think so. Here, take one."

He held out one of the swords, but I took a step back.

"I think I'll pass. Something tells me I would end up skewered if I tried to use that thing."

"Don't be a baby. Here." He shoved the sword into my hand.

The tip instantly hit the ground.

"This thing is heavy," I grumbled.

"It's a sword, not a feather. Now, hold it up," Cain said.

I grumbled under my breath as I held the sword up in front of me. "Happy?"

"Ecstatic. Now, I'm going to teach you how to use it. We'll start with blocking first."

I gaped at him. "Seriously? Why would I ever need to know how to use a sword?"

"We don't exactly have fighter jets and machine guns in Heaven and Hell. We fight with swords."

"I still don't understand how that has anything to do with me."

"You're being stalked by Death," he said, as if it were the most obvious thing in the world.

"And?"

He sighed. "You know, for someone so intelligent, you can be a bit dim-witted at times. Death isn't from this realm, Ella. The only thing you can use against him are weapons from the other realms. Since you're not an angel or demon, you have nothing to protect yourself with, except for these."

"The swords?" I asked.

"The swords," he agreed. "They're not from this realm, so that means they'll work against Death. Obviously, you can't kill him, but you can fend him off until Asher or I can get to you."

I looked down at the sword in my hand. It looked completely ordinary to me. The blade itself was wicked sharp. The hilt was made of polished wood.

"This sword came from Hell?"

"Yep. I brought both of them with me. You can never be too careful."

"I expected…more," I said. "Maybe some rubies on the handle, flames shooting out of it…something."

He laughed. It was genuine, not his usual cold laughter. "Sorry to disappoint, but Hell isn't much for dazzling mortals. I use these swords in battle. I don't showcase them."

"Oh," I said, feeling silly.

"Anyway, let's get started." Cain held up his own sword. "Like I said, I want to teach you how to block first."

"But Death doesn't have a sword," I pointed out.

"Just think of Death as one big sword. Block him with yours, and give yourself time to get away." He smirked. "Or time for us to come save you."

"What are you doing?" a voice demanded from behind me.

I spun around to see Asher standing at the bottom of the stairs, glaring at both of us.

"Asher, so glad you could join us," Cain said.

"I asked, what are you doing?" Asher stalked across the room to us.

Cain's smile never faltered. "I'm teaching Ella how to stay alive. Is that a problem?"

"You have no right, Cain! None at all. You keep pulling her deeper and deeper into all of this before it's time!" Asher shouted, surprising me.

"Time for what?" I asked.

Asher froze. He swallowed roughly as he looked anywhere but at me.

"Time for what?" I repeated.

"Oh dear, brother. I think you've put your foot in your mouth," Cain mused.

I ignored him as I stepped closer to Asher.

His gaze fell to the sword in my hand, and he automatically took a step back. "Keep that away from me."

"What are you hiding from me, Asher?"

His gaze finally found mine. "Nothing you need to worry about right now. You'll know soon enough."

"Why don't we show her how it's done?" Cain said after a moment of silence.

"What?" I looked over at him.

He held up his sword. "Give yours to Asher. We'll give you a demonstration."

"Like I'd touch a demon sword," Asher hissed.

"Oh, that's right. You're above me. I almost forgot." Cain's tone was arrogant, but there was a calculating look in his eyes.

"You know as well as I do that if I so much as prick my finger with that sword, I'm finished. I'm not a fool, Cain. Nothing you say will convince me to sign my own death certificate."

"One little prick would kill you?" I asked in disbelief.

He nodded. "Yes, and the same goes for Cain if he were injured by an angel's sword."

I looked down at the sword in my hand with newfound respect. "Wow."

"It just so happens that I have a sword of my own. Would you still like me to help you demonstrate?" Asher asked Cain.

Cain seemed surprised. "And where have you been hiding that little gem? I would've sensed it nearby, just like you sensed these."

Asher chuckled. "Some of us are a little smarter than others. We don't just leave things lying around."

Then, he vanished. It was so abrupt that even Cain seemed unsettled.

I sighed. It must be nice to just vanish whenever you felt like it. I knew I would've used that little trick several times over the past few months.

"I guess it's just you and me then," Cain said, turning back to me. "Are you ready?"

"Not really," I admitted as I held my sword up again.

"The first thing you need to do is relax," he pointed out.

"I'm in a basement with a demon who just happens to be holding a magical demon sword. I don't see myself relaxing anytime soon."

He snickered. "But I'm such a nice demon. You should know that by now."

"Oh, yes. You're as sweet as a kitten," I grumbled.

He placed his sword so that it was leaning against the wall, and then he walked around to stand behind me. My already tense body tightened up even more when his hands rested on my shoulders.

"Relax. Please."

I closed my eyes and forced myself to relax. I opened my eyes when Cain let go of me. I watched as he grabbed his sword and stopped to stand directly in front of me.

"Take a deep breath," he instructed. "Good. Now, let it out."

"Now what?" I asked.

"Spread your legs."

"Excuse me?" I asked in disbelief.

He rolled his eyes. "Spread your legs apart. Your feet need to be shoulder width apart, so you don't fall. Balance is important when you're holding a pointy object."

"Ha-ha." I moved my feet farther apart.

"Good. Now, hold your sword like this."

I watched as he lowered his hands so that they were even with his torso. The length of the sword ran up his body and stopped directly in front of his face. I mirrored his position, feeling a bit stupid.

"Perfect. Always try to maintain this position. It will protect you."

Cain seemed pleased with me so far. That was surprising.

"The next part—I want you to watch my every move. You're not learning how to fight. You only need to know how to block. Keep your eyes not only on my sword, but on my body as well. If I move left, adjust your stance accordingly. Make sure your elbows are bent, so you have more control. Plus, your sword will be closer to your body."

"Okay, let's do this," I said.

Cain's expression went from playful to serious in a split second. My natural instinct was to tense up, but I refrained. It was harder than I'd thought it would be. I carefully studied Cain, waiting for him to strike. He stayed very still, assessing me in the same way I did with him.

Finally, he moved. In a single moment, he went from completely still to swiveling his body and coming at me from the right. I turned my body toward him, but he was too fast. Before I could even think of blocking him, his sword was touching my side.

I cursed.

"Again," he demanded.

We moved back into our original positions once again and started over. Over and over again, his sword touched me. No matter how hard I tried, I couldn't match his speed. Cain was lethal. He knew it, and after an hour of getting pretend-stabbed, I knew it, too.

"This is pointless," I finally said. "I'm never going to be able to block you, Cain. You're too fast. What chance do I have against you?"

"If you think I'm bad, wait until Death corners you. He'll make me look like an old man with a walker."

I dropped my sword to the floor and sat down on the cold concrete. "Then, there's absolutely no hope for me."

"Maybe not, but the only thing you can do is continue to practice with me. You'll start to improve. Even after only an hour, you're already getting better."

I laughed, but there was no humor in it. "Yet you still stabbed me every time."

He shrugged. "I'm just that good."

I glared at him.

"Come on. Let's get something to eat. I'm starving." Cain picked my sword up off the floor and carried both of them back to the chest. He locked it before turning back to me. "How does pizza sound?" he asked.

My stomach rumbled. "My stomach seems to think it sounds perfect."

I followed him upstairs and sat on the couch while he ordered a pizza for us.

Once it arrived, we ate in silence. I expected Asher to appear at any moment, shooting glares at Cain, but he never did.

In fact, I didn't see him for the rest of the week.

Eighteen

"Amanda! Amanda, wait!" I called out the next morning as soon as Cain and I spotted Amanda.

She had turned to leave when she saw us moving toward her, but she stopped when she heard me.

I glanced over at Cain. "I need you to give us a few minutes."

"Why?" he asked.

"So, I can clean up the mess you made yesterday," I said.

He frowned. "Fine, but stay within sight. I'm going to try to find my idiot brother."

I headed in Amanda's direction, afraid that she'd disappear if I didn't hurry.

"Hey," I said when I reached her.

"Hi." Her tone was emotionless.

I winced. It was like the past six months had never even happened. She acted like she didn't even know me.

"Can we talk?" I asked.

She shrugged. "I guess."

I took her arm and led her over to a row of empty seats. I sat down, pulling her down with me.

"You didn't answer when I tried to call you last night," I said.

She shrugged again. "I was busy."

I sighed. "Right. Anyway, I just wanted to apologize for what happened yesterday."

"What happened? You have a new boyfriend and didn't even bother to tell me. I couldn't care less," she said.

"That's a lie, Amanda. You do care. I want to explain why I didn't tell you." When she didn't speak, I continued, "Asher and I aren't exactly together. Cain exaggerated a little bit."

"What do you mean?"

"I don't know what's going on between Asher and me. We're still trying to figure it out."

"Why didn't you at least tell me that?" she asked. She didn't try to hide the hurt in her voice this time. "We're all each other has. I thought we told each other everything."

"I never had the chance to tell you. Asher was constantly around us. Plus, it scares me a little, you know? Ever since…" I hesitated. "Ever since my mom went nuts, I've been so lost. You've helped me, and for that, I'll be forever grateful. Now that Cain and Asher are here, it feels like things are getting even harder for me. I'm scared that I'm going to get hurt by one or even both of them."

I realized just how true my words were. Cain and Asher were now a huge part of my life. Even though I wanted to smack them most days, I was starting to care for both of them. I had no idea what to do with that. Once this was all over, both of them would have to leave. I'd be just as alone as I was before their abrupt invasion of my life. That thought scared me more than I wanted to admit. I was getting attached. In my situation, that was the dumbest thing I could possibly do.

"So, you're not really with Asher?" Amanda asked, pulling me from my thoughts.

"I don't know what's going on with either of them, Amanda. That's the truth. The only thing I can tell you is that I feel a connection with both of them."

Amanda cracked a grin. "Both of them, huh? Can I just say that I think you're officially involved in the hottest love triangle since…well, ever."

I rolled my eyes. "There's no love triangle. I promise. Things are much more complicated than that."

"Care to elaborate?" she asked.

"I wish I could, but I can't." When I saw hurt flash through her eyes, I hurried on to say, "I would tell you everything if it was my secret to tell, but it's not. I'm sorry for that."

She frowned. "I thought you decided to start keeping things from me because you didn't want to be friends anymore. I assumed you were going to replace me with Cain and Asher. I was stupid to think that."

I gently hugged her. "I could never replace you, Amanda. You've stuck by me when everyone else abandoned me. You're what a true friend really is."

She hugged me back. "Sorry I got all huffy. It won't happen again. I promise."

"It'd better not because if you leave me alone with those two, I'll strangle you myself."

We sat together until the first bell sounded. I spotted Cain across the room. He headed toward us with a frown on his face. He joined us as we started walking down the hallway. He responded when Amanda greeted him, but other than that, he stayed silent.

Once we left Amanda at her locker, I turned to him. "Did you find Asher?"

He shook his head. "Nope, which leaves us with a problem. You're going to be alone all morning."

"I'll be fine," I said as I started up the stairs.

"I'll keep an eye on you," Cain said when we reached the top.

"How?" I asked.

He grinned as he glanced around the hallway. I looked around, too. There were only a few students, and none of them were looking at us.

"What are you going—" I stopped talking when I realized that Cain wasn't standing in front of me anymore.

"Of course. You're going to go all invisible man on me, so you can stalk me in the bathroom," I said. "Have fun with that. I won't be going anywhere near a bathroom today."

He didn't reappear to respond, not that I'd expected him to. I sighed as I walked to my locker and tossed my things inside. It creeped me out to know that Cain was with me even though I couldn't see him. I wondered how many times in my life I had been watched by an angel or demon without even knowing. Their little disappearing act was disturbing, to say the least.

I quickly walked to class, pretending that I didn't have an invisible demon somewhere close by. I did groan out loud when I walked into history and saw Stacey was already there, waving at me.

"Morning, Ella," she chirped.

I nodded, hoping that she'd take the hint and leave me alone. Of course, that wasn't going to happen.

"So, I heard that you're with Asher Collins. Is it true?" she asked before I could sit down.

I shrugged. "It's complicated."

She laughed. "With the way he looks, I don't see how it could be."

I glared. "You know, there's a lot more to Cain and Asher than just their looks."

"Like what?"

"Never mind," I said as Mrs. Carpenter walked in. There was no way I could say a word about either of them without Cain giving me crap about it later.

"Well, since you're with Asher, you should introduce me to Cain," Stacey said, ignoring the fact that class was starting.

"You don't want to meet him," I whispered.

"I promise you that I do. I mean, have you seen the boy?" She giggled. "Of course you have. You're dating his twin."

"Miss Winston, is there something you'd like to share with the class?" Mrs. Carpenter asked.

Stacey turned around. "Nope. I was just talking to Ella about our homework," she lied.

Mrs. Carpenter didn't look convinced, but she turned her attention back to the chalkboard.

I sighed in relief when Stacey didn't turn back around. From my right, I swore I could hear Cain laughing.

The rest of the day was uneventful. Amanda seemed to be back to her usual self. Cain decided to reappear around lunchtime. The three of us sat together at lunch. I continued to search the room for Asher, but he was nowhere to be seen. When Amanda asked where he was, Cain lied and told her that he was out sick. By the end of the day, he still hadn't made an appearance. I was starting to get worried.

"Do you think he's okay?" I asked Cain once we made it back to my house.

"Who?" he asked.

"Seriously?" I asked. "Your brother. You know, the one we haven't seen since last night."

"Oh, him. I'm sure he's fine. He's probably off somewhere singing with a choir or rescuing stray animals. Maybe he's feeding a starving village in Africa."

"You're not funny," I seethed. "This is serious, Cain, and you know it. Asher wouldn't just up and disappear like this."

He shrugged. "Maybe he was summoned."

"Summoned?" I asked.

"Yeah, summoned, as in the big, bad boss wanted to see him."

"Oh, I never even thought of that. Do you guys get summoned a lot?"

"I don't know about him, but I rarely get summoned. I'm sure I will soon though since I'm not on a normal job."

"That sounds…fun," I said after a moment.

He smirked. "Yeah, it's a bucket of laughs."

"What happens if you get summoned while Asher is gone?"

"I hand you a sword and wish you the best of luck until I get back." He frowned. "Speaking of swords, let's get started on your training again. Homework can wait."

I sighed.

Spending the entire week with Cain following me everywhere grated on my nerves. The fact that he seemed to enjoy tormenting me didn't help either. I tried to ignore his sarcastic remarks and constant flow of innuendos, but it was hard. Most of the time, I kept my cool by imagining locking him in a room that he couldn't escape from or hitting him really hard. Whenever I pictured that, he would always ask what I was smiling about.

By the time Friday evening rolled around, I was ready to hand deliver myself to Death just to escape Cain.

"What am I supposed to do tonight while you work?" Cain grumbled from my bed.

I glanced over to see him lying on top of my sheets like he owned them.

"You could always make yourself invisible and go watch one of the movies." I grabbed my coat off my chair.

"While I'd prefer to do that, I can't. I have to keep you within sight, remember?"

I sighed. "Cain, seriously, I've showered and peed several times this week without you around. Death hasn't made an appearance. I think I'll be safe while I'm working. Besides, I'll be surrounded by people all night. He isn't going to kill me while I make popcorn."

"I won't take that chance. If Asher comes back to find you dead, he'll kill me—again."

"Have you heard anything at all from him?" I asked for the hundredth time.

While Cain seemed unconcerned about Asher's abrupt disappearance, I was starting to seriously worry that I'd never see him again.

"Nope, and I don't expect to. If he was summoned, there's no way he'll be able to contact me."

"What if he wasn't summoned? What if he just...left? I mean, he was really upset the last time we saw him."

Cain sat up. "Ella, there's no way that he can just walk away from an assignment. I can't either. It doesn't matter how angry I make him. He's stuck with me."

"And what if they pulled him from his *assignment*?" I asked.

"They won't. They're too curious. Plus, they'd never let him walk away when you also have a demon on your tail."

I glanced at the clock. "I need to head to work if I want to make it there on time."

He stood. "Fine, let's go."

Annoyed, I followed him out of my room and down the stairs. I stopped in the living room to let Uncle Jack know that I was leaving before continuing out the front door. I ignored Cain as I walked to my own car and climbed in.

"Don't you want to take my ride?" He climbed into the passenger seat.

"Nope. I don't get off work until midnight. It'll be too cold to ride around on a motorcycle," I told him as I started my car.

He groaned in defeat and slumped against his seat. "You're absolutely no fun, Ella. I hope you know that."

"I'm aware." I backed out of my driveway and pulled onto the main road.

I lovingly patted my steering wheel, glad to be driving my own car again.

Uncle Jack had finally remembered to call his friend to fix my car last Thursday. He'd discovered the alternator was bad. I'd cringed when I stopped by the parts store to buy a new one. It had taken a massive chunk out of my savings, but I needed a car. I knew my uncle would have paid for the part, but I hadn't wanted him to. He'd already done so much for me. Plus, I felt bad for the way Asher had messed with his head.

As I drove to work, Cain constantly flipped through the radio channels. He seemed intolerant to commercials.

"That's annoying," I finally said.

"You're annoying, yet I'm still forced to deal with you," he shot back.

I pressed my lips together to keep from starting another verbal war with him. It wasn't worth the energy. Instead, I stayed silent until we finally arrived at the movie theater where I worked. I circled the lot until I found a spot to park in.

There wasn't a lot to do around Shinnston, so most teenagers would spend a lot of their time in the theaters and in the mall that was connected to it. That meant that most of the time, my shifts at work would fly by. I hoped tonight wouldn't be any different.

Nineteen

As soon as I parked my car, I climbed out and locked it. Cain followed me across the lot to the sidewalk.

"You might want to go invisible now unless you feel like explaining to everyone I work with why you're following me around," I said as I turned to look at him.

He smirked at me before disappearing.

I stared at the spot where I knew he was still standing. Curious, I reached out to see if I could feel him. I moved my hand back and forth, unable to touch anything but air.

"I guess I don't have to worry about anyone bumping into you tonight," I finally said before turning and walking inside.

Several people were standing in line in the lobby. I moved past them and walked through the door marked *Employees Only*. After shoving my coat and purse into my locker and locking it, I clocked in. Resigned to my fate of shoving popcorn into containers for the next six hours, I walked through another door that led to the counter.

My manager, Colton, smiled when he saw me. "Hey, Ella. I want you at the ticket counter for a while."

"Sure." I walked over to where he was standing.

He was ringing through a couple of girls who were buying tickets to the latest romantic comedy. Once he finished with them, he logged out and moved away, so I could get logged into the system.

For the next four hours, I did nothing but ring people through. Friday nights were always busy, but this one was ridiculous. For a while, I forgot that I had a demon in the lobby with me, watching out for Death, who seemed determined to find me. For just a few hours, I felt normal.

"Ella, you can take a break. I'll run the ticket counter while you're gone," Colton said after walking over to me.

"Thanks." I felt dead on my feet. My stomach rumbled, reminding me that I hadn't taken the time to eat before coming to work. "I think I'll grab something from the food court. I'll be back in fifteen."

He nodded as I walked away. I clocked out and headed out through the employee door and into the lobby. I was relieved to see that it was finally starting to clear out a little.

The mall was directly connected to the theater, but to move from one building to the other, I had to walk outside. It wasn't far, but it was annoying when it was cold out. I hurried through the exit door and down the sidewalk to the nearest mall entrance. The temperature had dropped significantly since I arrived for work. I hoped that it didn't start snowing before I made it home. My poor car probably wouldn't make it since the tires were practically bald.

"Are you going to buy me something, too? I'm starving," Cain said from beside me.

I yelped in surprise, causing several people to turn and look at me.

My face heated in embarrassment as I turned to glare at Cain. "A little warning would be nice when we're in public you know."

"That wouldn't be nearly as fun." He grinned as he held the door open for me. "And you didn't answer my original question, so I'm taking that as a yes. Can we grab some mall pizza?"

"Buy your own," I huffed as I started walking across the mall.

Our mall was fairly simple compared to some I'd heard of. It was only one story with one large open space going through the entire place. The food court was down a hallway right in the center of the mall.

Worried that there would be a line, I quickened my pace. Cain stayed silent as we walked together. I caught several girls looking in our direction, their gazes focused on Cain.

At school, most of the girls had finally settled down over the Collins brothers. I'd forgotten what it was like when strangers met either of them. They made every single person in the room stop and take notice. I wasn't sure if it was some kind of demon charisma that helped Cain or if he'd always been this way. I didn't dare ask him, not wanting to inflate his ego even more.

When we reached the food court, Cain grabbed my hand and tugged me over to the pizza shop. I glanced down at my hand in his. Since Asher had disappeared, Cain seemed to find more and more reasons to touch me. I wasn't sure how I felt about that. He had kissed me twice, but that was before I had known what he really was. Things had changed since then, and I'd made it clear that I didn't want him to kiss me again. He hadn't tried again. Instead, he constantly found reasons to touch me.

I stayed silent as Cain ordered two slices of pizza and drinks for us. I raised an eyebrow when I saw him paying for both of us as well. Whenever Cain was genuinely nice, it always surprised me.

He handed me the drinks to carry before grabbing the pizza and finding a nearby table to sit down at. I sat across from him. When he slid my paper plate across the table, I picked it up and started eating like a woman possessed.

"Hungry?" he teased.

I nodded, my mouth too full to speak.

"We only have two more hours until you're free, right?" he asked.

I nodded again.

"Good. When we get home, I want to practice with the swords some more. You're really starting to improve."

I gave him a look of disbelief as I swallowed my food. "We won't get home until well after midnight. You can't really want to practice tonight. It'll be too late."

"You need all the practice you can get."

"My uncle—" I started to argue but stopped.

"Your uncle will look the other way, just like he always does, thanks to Asher."

I grumbled under my breath as I took another bite. I hated to admit it, but Cain was right. I did need to practice.

Over the past week, I had improved greatly, but it wasn't enough, not even close. I was proud of the fact that I'd managed to block him once last night. He'd seemed as surprised as I was over that. The sword was starting to feel more comfortable in my hand, not so heavy and awkward.

Cain had seemed to think that I was capable of handling it on my own if Death appeared. We had stashed my sword under my bed last Tuesday night. He'd given me strict instructions not to touch it unless we were practicing or if Death decided to visit me.

As we ate, I people-watched. Friday night at the mall was always guaranteed to bring out a few oddballs. Once, I'd even seen a man dressed up in a gorilla suit while his companion wore a banana costume. Tonight though, I didn't see anyone out of the ordinary.

A few tables down from us was a young woman with her toddler son. She was trying to coax him into eating, but all he wanted to do was play with his toys.

A couple sat close by as well. They were leaning across the table toward each other. The man was talking too low for me to hear, but whatever he was saying made the woman smile and blush.

Teenagers walked past us in groups—the boys trying to look tough, the girls glued to their every word.

For a moment, I wished I were one of them. Everyone around me was normal. They were out, living their normal lives, doing normal things with their normal friends. They had no idea that there was a demon nearby, devouring pizza, as he watched over a girl who everyone seemed to want dead.

"What are you thinking?" Cain asked, pulling me out of my trance.

I shook my head. "Nothing really. Just..." I motioned to the crowd around us. "That was me six months ago, Cain. I had friends. I was normal. Now, everything is so confusing. I'm no longer just an average girl. I'm a freak. And the worst part? I don't even understand why I'm a freak. I don't get why my mother tried to kill me—*twice*. I don't understand why Death seems so interested in me. What did I do to deserve all of this?"

I was on the verge of tears, but I held them back. Crying would do nothing but make me look weak in Cain's eyes. I didn't want that. I wanted him to see me as more than just a girl who had caused him so many problems.

"Hey, look at me," Cain said.

I looked up to see him watching me with a serious expression on his face.

"You didn't *do* anything, Ella. Sometimes, fate has more in store for us than others. You're special, Ella. You're going to do amazing things. These people around us? They won't. They'll live out their lives like everyone else. They won't do anything special. It's them who you should be feeling sorry for. You're going to experience so much more than any of them could ever imagine."

"What are you talking about?" I asked, confused.

He shook his head. "Nothing. I just meant that you should accept whatever happens next. Fate has already set things in motion for you. You were picked for this."

I stayed quiet for a moment. "I know you're hiding something from me, Cain. I'm not an idiot." He opened his mouth, but I held up my hand. "I'm not going to ask you what it is you're hiding—not yet anyway. I get that you and Asher both have rules that you have to follow. I won't get you in trouble. I can wait. I just…I hope that whatever it is will help me. I don't want to go any deeper into whatever this is than I already am."

"I'm truly sorry, Ella, but I can't tell you anything that will ease your mind—not now at least." He reached across the table and took my hand in his. "When all of this is over, you'll understand just how special you really are."

I closed my eyes as his warm hand covered mine. I wanted more than anything to turn my hand over and lace my fingers through his. That was so incredibly wrong. Even worse was the way I felt when Cain acted this way. He was a safe haven for me. It scared me to realize just how much I had started to care for him. Even when he annoyed me, I was fond of him. When he left, I was going to be devastated. The same went for Asher. Both of these boys had wormed their way into my life, and I wasn't sure I'd ever truly be ready to let them go.

Cain pulled away. "We'd better head back, or you'll be late."

My eyes snapped open, and I felt my face flush in embarrassment. I quickly finished my food before standing and tossing my garbage in the trash can next to our table.

Cain stayed in sight until just before we walked back into the theater. Out of the corner of my eye, I saw him disappear.

When I made it back to the counter, Colton was no longer standing behind the register. He had one of the other girls, Shelly, running the ticket register. Confused, I made my way back through the employee doors.

Colton was standing on the other side, waiting for me. "Ella, I want you to start cleaning the empty theaters. Nine and six just let out. Start with them," he said. His voice sounded strange. It lacked any kind of emotion at all.

Instantly, I went on high alert. "Uh...sure. Is everything okay? I thought I was on register tonight," I said.

"Clean six and nine, Ella." Then, he turned and walked away, leaving me alone in the room.

"That seem odd to you?" I asked Cain, knowing that he was with me.

He appeared in front of me. "Yeah, definitely. If I didn't know any better, I would guess that an angel or a demon has tampered with his memory."

"What?" My voice was full of surprise.

He nodded. "Yeah. If it's a demon, I'm not worried, but an angel concerns me. Most of them aren't like Asher. They won't just play nice for the sake of the job. There's a good chance that they'll see me and pull out one of their shiny little swords."

"Wonderful," I muttered. "Stay close I guess. If it's an angel, leave before they have a chance to hurt you."

He chuckled. "Angels don't scare me, Ella. I have yet to meet one who can win against me."

"Don't be cocky," I snapped. "That could very well be your downfall one day."

He rolled his eyes before disappearing again. I shook my head in annoyance as I walked back out into the lobby and headed toward the theater's entrance. I made my way down the hallway to the supply closet. I flipped on the light, half-expecting someone to be waiting for me. The room was empty. I loaded up a cart with cleaning supplies and tugged it out of the closet. It caught on the rug, nearly toppling over.

"You could help you know," I grumbled to Cain.

He didn't reappear, and the cart didn't start moving, so I assumed that meant I was on my own.

Cursing the carpeted floor, I pushed the cart down to theater six. I opened the door and held it open with my hip as I struggled to push the cart inside.

"You're so weak, little mortal," Cain said as he appeared behind the cart.

"Thanks," I said when he pushed it through the doorway. I grabbed the cleaning sign off of the cart and put it outside the door before letting it close softly behind me.

"Will there be anyone in here?" Cain whispered as he helped me push the cart up the ramp.

"There shouldn't be, but if I were you, I'd hide until we're sure."

"Have fun with the cart then." He disappeared from sight.

The cart lunged backward since he wasn't helping me push. I dug my heels into the ground to keep if from rolling all the way back down to the entrance.

"Stupid demons," I grumbled. "And stupid carts. This is why I hate cleaning duty."

Normally, the guys I worked with were assigned to cleaning duty since most of them were bigger than any of the girls. Also, they usually worked in pairs to get the job done faster. That made me extra leery of being sent in here to clean on my own.

As I pushed the cart the rest of the way up the ramp, my eyes darted around to what I could see of the room. Even with the lights on the walls, there were still areas that I couldn't see. I stopped once I reached the end of the ramp, relieved that I'd made it to the top.

The theater was split into two sections, and I stood in the middle. Below me were twenty or so rows of seats and the ginormous screen. Above me were even more seats and the small projection window. I looked around the theater, still searching for someone about to jump out at me.

"Up here," a voice called from the top of the rows.

I froze for a moment before I finally realized who it was.

"Cain, you're an ass. Don't scare me like that!" I grumbled.

"That wasn't me," Cain said as he appeared a few feet away from me. His eyes were trained on the figure who had spoken.

"Wha—Asher?" I called out.

Asher slowly moved out of the shadows and made his way down the steps toward us. Without stopping to think, I rushed up the stairs to meet him. I hurdled myself into his arms, causing him to make an *umph* sound as he was forced to take a step back.

"I guess it's safe to say that you're happy to see me," he murmured against my hair. "If I had known I'd receive this kind of greeting, I would have tried to get back sooner."

I pulled away. Now that I knew he was safe, I was annoyed that he'd just disappeared without telling us that he was leaving.

I glared at him. "And just where have you been for the past week? I was worried sick about you!"

He frowned. "I'm sorry. If I could have told you I had to leave, I would have. They didn't give me a chance though. They pulled me back without summoning me."

"Why would they do that?" Cain spoke up finally.

I glanced back to see him walking up the steps toward us. He stopped a few stairs away and leaned against the wall. "Usually, if they pull you back without a summons, you don't come back. Most of the time, it means you're in deep shit."

Asher looked over my head at Cain. "They didn't pull me back because I did something wrong. They needed to speak with me."

"And summoning you wasn't an option?"

Asher hesitated. "They needed to talk to me immediately."

"Interesting," Cain murmured. "I'm curious, what exactly did they need to speak with you about?"

Asher glanced down at me before meeting Cain's gaze again. "We'll talk about it soon, but right now isn't the time."

"Because I'm here?" I asked.

Asher nodded. "I'm sorry, Ella, but yes. I can't talk to you about this, not yet."

"More secrets. Just what I need," I said, not bothering to hide my annoyance.

"I will tell you but not yet. I have my orders, and I can't ignore them yet again. They're angry with me already."

"For what?" I asked.

"For telling you the truth about what I am. They…made me understand that it wouldn't end well if I went against them again."

"They tortured you?" Cain's voice was sharp.

When Asher didn't answer, I gasped in horror. "They did, didn't they?"

"It doesn't matter. Just let it go, both of you," Asher said.

Anger surged through my veins. "How dare they hurt you for telling me the truth! I wish I could hurt every single one of them. Heaven is supposed to be filled with the good ones." I laughed, but it held no humor. "I think I hate them. No, I'm sure of it."

"Don't say that!" Asher snapped. "You don't hate them, Ella. Don't you dare even think that."

"Why not?" Cain asked. There was smugness in his tone that I didn't like. "Afraid she'll decide that Hell is the better team?"

"Enough, both of you," I said as I looked back and forth between the two of them. "You're back, Asher. That's all that matters."

"It feels good to be back here with you." Asher smiled down at me.

His expression was so sincere that my anger over his abrupt departure started to disappear.

"Not to spoil a super special moment between the two of you, but I think Ella should get back to work before someone walks in here and notices her standing here, talking to us," Cain said, killing the moment.

I fought not to roll my eyes. "You're right, I suppose. Sticky soda isn't going to mop itself up."

"I'll help you," Asher said. "With both of us working, it won't take very long."

"I'll just sit down somewhere and watch you two work," Cain said.

"Why don't you take the rest of the night off?" Asher asked. "You've been with Ella nonstop for an entire week. I'm sure you could use some time to yourself."

Cain chuckled. "You forget that I know you better than myself, Asher. I think I'll stick around for a while."

"No, it's okay, really. You could use some alone time," I said. "I know you hate following me around, and you had to do it for a week straight. Go enjoy yourself for a while."

Cain frowned. "You both want to get rid of me that badly?"

"I didn't say I wanted to get rid of you," I told him. "I just know you. You're probably dying to get away from me."

"It's settled then. We'll see you later, Cain," Asher spoke up before Cain could.

Cain rolled his eyes. "I guess I could go watch cable porn for a bit. That'll be more entertaining than watching you two I suppose." He looked at Asher. "I take it, we'll be talking later?"

Asher glanced at me before nodding. "Yeah. I'll find you."

"You won't have to look far. I'll be in my bedroom, enjoying my break." His tone was full of sarcasm. He flipped us off before disappearing.

"Typical Cain," I muttered.

Asher laughed. "Would you have him any other way?"

I shook my head. "No. Not that I'd ever admit this to him, but he's starting to grow on me a bit." I winced. "I probably should have given him time to actually leave in case he decided to go all invisible instead of leaving."

Asher grinned. "Don't worry. He's really gone, so your secret is safe with me."

"Good." I smiled up at him. "I really am glad that you're back. I didn't realize how accustomed I've become to having you around."

"I'm starting to grow on you, too, huh?" he teased.

"Maybe just a little," I said. "I suppose we should get started on cleaning before someone comes in to check on me and realizes I've done absolutely nothing."

I started to turn and walk back down the stairs to where my cart waited for me, but Asher reached out and grabbed my arm to stop me.

"Ella, wait." He stepped down so that we were on the same level. "I…I did a lot of thinking while I was away." His tone turned serious, instantly putting me on guard.

"About what?"

"You."

I raised an eyebrow. "Me? What about me?"

He raised his hand so that it cupped my cheek. His thumb moved back and forth across my skin, leaving tingles as it went. "I've always been the one to follow the rules without question. I've never let my emotions get in the way of my goal—until you. While I was up there, I kept thinking, what if the next time I leave, I never see you again? I would always regret…"

"Regret what?" I asked after a moment of silence.

"I would always regret not doing this." He leaned forward.

Before I could utter a word, his lips pressed against mine. I was so surprised that all I could do was stand there for a moment. Finally, my brain started working again. My lips moved against Asher's, timidly at first. Then, I lost all inhibitions and kissed him properly. Our lips melded together over and over again as Asher wrapped his arms around me and tightly pulled me against him. Lost in the moment, I threw my arms around his neck and clung to him.

A part of me, a very tiny part, told me that this was wrong. It was *Asher*. He was my friend. He was also Cain's brother and an angel.

Guilt started to worm its way into my perfect moment, and I forced myself to pull away. I gasped the moment we broke contact, suddenly ashamed of what I was doing.

"I had to do that just once, Ella. I hope you'll forgive me," Asher said quietly. His cheeks were tinged pink, almost as if he were embarrassed over what he'd just done.

"Asher…" I started, but I couldn't think of the right thing to say. My mind was too filled with not only guilt, but with happiness as well. I realized that I'd wished for Asher to kiss me for a long time. I just couldn't bring myself to admit it.

"Don't say anything, please. Just let it go," Asher said quietly. "I'm sorry that I made you do that."

That caught my attention. "*Made me?* You didn't make me do anything, Asher. I kissed you back freely."

"You're ashamed now. I can sense it." His voice was defeated.

"I'm not ashamed of kissing *you*, you idiot. I'm ashamed that I've kissed both you and your brother. That…that alone makes me a horrible person. Add in the fact that one of you is a demon and the other an angel and…well, yeah, no words."

Asher gaped at me. "That's all?"

"All?" I practically shouted. "You're brothers, Asher! *Brothers.*"

He laughed as if I'd just said the funniest thing he'd ever heard. "Oh, Ella. You don't need to feel guilty over Cain. He doesn't…how do I put this, so I don't insult you? Cain has never taken women seriously. Never. When he kissed you, he didn't mean anything by it.

More than likely, he did it just to mess with your head. Kissing Cain doesn't even count as kissing."

"That makes no sense," I said.

"But it does. If you feel like you're betraying both of us, you shouldn't. I promise you that Cain wouldn't feel betrayed if he knew that you just kissed me. I certainly don't feel that way."

"When I admitted that I kissed him the day that you finally told me what you were, you looked upset," I said, not fully believing him.

"I was, but only because I was worried you would see it as more and side with him."

I sat down on the step as I tried to collect my thoughts. "So, Cain did it just to tease me."

"More than likely, yes," Asher answered.

I thought back to the day that Cain had kissed me.

"What are you doing to me?" He released me and stepped away.

"What was that supposed to mean? I didn't do anything! You kissed me," I said.

"Yeah, I know. Damn it, Ella. I didn't plan that. Nothing has gone according to plan since I got here, and it's all because of you."

His words made me think that Asher was wrong. Cain had been bothered by the fact that he'd kissed me. If he were only doing it to tease me or draw me in closer, he wouldn't have reacted like that. Or would he have? Cain seemed to be a professional at manipulating me.

Since I'd discovered the truth about the brothers, Cain hadn't made a move at all. Maybe he was worried that I would reject him because of what he was, or maybe Asher was telling the truth. Either way, the whole situation was messed up.

"Let's get this place cleaned," Asher said as he reached down and gripped my upper arm, pulling me to my feet. "We can talk about everything else later."

I just nodded, too lost inside my own head to even speak.

It seemed that things were growing more and more complicated when it came to the Collins brothers and me.

Twenty

A sher didn't mention my kiss with either of them for the rest of the night. Instead, he talked about anything else that seemed to pop into his head. By the time my shift ended and we were driving home, I had started to tune him out.

When we pulled into my driveway, I realized that he was no longer speaking. I glanced over at him as he climbed out of the car. I couldn't help but wonder what I was going to do with them. Somehow, over the last few weeks, I'd come to realize that I cared for both of them. After Asher's kiss, I now knew that I felt more than just friendship for him. Even with Cain and all the uncertainty surrounding him, I knew I cared for him too much as well.

"They're going to be the death of me," I mumbled as I climbed out of the car.

"What?" Asher asked.

I shook my head as we started walking up to my house. "Nothing. I was just thinking out loud."

When we walked inside, I kicked off my shoes and headed upstairs. I stopped and checked on Uncle Jack to make sure he was sleeping before heading to my room. Asher followed me every step of the way.

Inside my room, I dropped my purse onto my desk and walked to my dresser. Asher sat down on my computer chair and watched me as I searched for a pair of sweatpants and a T-shirt to sleep in.

"I'm going to go change in the bathroom. No need to follow me over there," I told him as I walked across the room, my pajamas clutched tightly in my hand.

I was slightly disappointed when he didn't come off with some sarcastic remark about helping me. I had to remind myself that it was Asher in my room now, not Cain. After a week of dealing with Cain and his antics, it would take a bit to get used to quiet Asher.

Across the hall, I changed quickly, washed my face, and tied my hair back into a loose ponytail. Satisfied, I headed back into my room.

Asher was still sitting in the chair. I wasn't even sure if he had moved.

"Can you stop being so…still? All the way home, you kept talking. Now, it's like you're a statue."

"I was trying to lessen the tension all evening. That's why I kept talking. When I realized you weren't even listening, I gave up," Asher said. "And sorry about being so…me. After a week in Heaven, it's hard to remember to act like a mortal."

"You weren't like this when we first met. Besides staring at me a lot, you acted fine."

He glanced away. "Uh…well, we were around you a bit before then."

I froze. "Wait, what?"

"Before we showed ourselves to you, we were ordered to watch you for anything unusual."

"So, basically, the two of you had orders to stalk me," I said. "You did your invisible trick, right?"

He nodded. "Yes."

"You weren't, like…in my room and stuff, were you?" When he didn't answer, I growled, "You can't be serious!"

"I'm sorry, Ella. We had our orders. Don't worry though. We didn't do anything to invade your privacy."

I laughed humorlessly. "Like watch me in private? Of course not. My room has all kinds of visitors."

"Like follow you to the shower," he said.

"You guys are unbelievable," I muttered. It creeped me out to think of them standing in my room, silently watching my every move.

"We had—"

"Yeah, yeah. Orders, I know," I said, cutting him off. "I think I'd like to go to bed now, Asher. Good night."

Angry and determined not to talk to him anymore, I flipped off my overhead light and climbed into bed. Without another word, I closed my eyes and shut Asher out. For several minutes, I forced myself to keep my breathing even while I listened for any kind of movement from Asher. Just when I was about to give up and really go to sleep, the computer chair he was sitting in squeaked.

"Ella?" Asher whispered. When I didn't answer, he sighed. "If you're awake, I'll be back soon. I need to talk to Cain."

For several moments after that, I listened intently for any sound at all. When I heard nothing, I slowly peeled my eyes open and looked around.

I was alone.

Without a second thought, I threw my covers off and stood. I needed to know what Asher was going to tell Cain. He wasn't allowed to tell me, but if I accidentally heard, surely, he wouldn't end up in trouble again.

Faster than I thought possible, I made it downstairs and out the front door. I didn't even stop to put shoes on, something I instantly regretted as I stepped out onto the frost-covered lawn. Too worried that I'd miss the conversation, I ran across the lawn to the front of Cain and Asher's house.

Carefully, I turned the handle, and the front door swung open without a sound. I held my breath as I walked to the stairs and tiptoed to the top of them. Amazed at my luck so far, I inched down the hallway to Cain's room.

The door was open with light spilling through. I stopped a foot or so away to avoid being spotted. I could hear Cain and Asher talking inside, but I couldn't make out what they were saying. I crept a bit closer until I was inches away from the door.

I held my breath and listened.

"So, what was so important that you needed to talk to me about it? Doesn't Heaven like to guard its secrets?" Cain's voice floated out into the hallway.

"Stop playing around, Cain. You can toss insults at me when I'm finished." Asher's voice was strained.

Cain sighed. "Fine. What's going on?"

"We're out of time."

"What do you mean?" Cain's voice had turned serious.

"What I said. We're out of time, Cain—both of us."

"How can you be sure?"

"A prophecy. That's why Heaven called me back. They wanted me to know."

"Why didn't Hell call me back, too, then?" Cain asked.

"I don't know. Maybe they were afraid to leave her alone with Death constantly hovering so close."

"How long?"

There was a pause before Asher spoke, "Three Earth days."

The room filled with silence. I stood completely still, terrified that they'd heard me and were going to catch me.

"I thought we had more time!" Cain finally said. "At least another month or two."

"I did, too, but something has changed. I wish I knew what," Asher said. "We can't tell her, Cain. I hope you know that. It would devastate her, and she's already been through enough. Let her enjoy what little time she has."

What little time I have? What's that supposed to mean?

"I'm not a fool, Asher. I won't tell Ella about her own death. Even I'm not that much of a dick."

Time froze. The air seemed to disappear from the hallway.

"Three Earth days."

"I won't tell Ella about her own death."

Surely, they weren't standing in Cain's room, talking about how long I had to live. Anger blazed through my body.

Had they known all along that I was supposed to die?

They had mentioned that they thought they had more time. That must mean that they had to have known. All those times I'd talked about the future with either of them, they'd known all along that I wouldn't even have one. From what they were saying now, I wouldn't even graduate, let alone leave this town behind.

Not caring about what happened next, I stepped into the light spilling from Cain's room. The brothers looked up as soon as I appeared.

Asher looked devastated. Even Cain wasn't smiling.

"Why didn't you tell me?" I asked.

"Ella," Cain said as he started to walk across the room to where I was standing.

I shook my head. "No, no more lies or half-truths. You two have known all along that I was going to die. Why didn't you tell me? Why did you pretend to protect me from Death?"

"We didn't pretend to protect you, Ella. We have been keeping him away from you." Asher said.

"Why? So, I can die at the right moment?" My voice was eerily calm—so much so, that I was starting to freak myself out.

"Death taking an interest in you was never part of the prophecy. We have no idea why he keeps trying to get to you ahead of schedule. We're still trying to figure it out."

"Why are you two really here? I want the truth this time," I said.

"We're here to watch over you," Asher said.

"Stop lying!" I shouted, finally losing my temper. "All either of you have done is lie to me since I met you!"

Cain took another step forward but stopped dead. His eyes were wide with surprise. It took me a moment to realize why.

The room had suddenly gone cold.

Death.

Asher started moving toward me, but he stopped a few feet away. A look of disbelief crossed his face. I watched as he tried to move forward, only to be blocked by some invisible barrier. He raised his hands and pushed at the force holding him back. Asher looked like a mime trying to escape his box. When he pushed, it was as if he was pushing on clear glass.

I would've laughed if it wasn't for the fact that Death was near.

"Ella, come here!" Cain shouted.

I tore my eyes away from Asher and ran to where they stood. When I tried to push through the barrier, I couldn't. It was like trying to walk through a brick wall.

"I can't!" I cried as I looked back and forth between the brothers.

As one, their gazes turned to something behind me. Asher went white and started struggling even harder against the barrier. Cain moved over to where I was standing and raised his hand so that it touched the barrier in the same spot as my hand.

"I'm so sorry, Ella," he said. He sounded defeated, which was even more terrifying than knowing the Death was standing behind me.

I tried to smile at him, but I failed. "It's all right. I'm sorry I was so angry with both of you. I just wanted to understand."

"I know," he said simply.

Taking a deep breath, I slowly turned around.

Death stood in the doorway, his cloak moving in time with an invisible breeze only he could feel.

"Ella, come to me." His voice filled the room, but only I seemed to hear it.

Determined to be brave, I walked across the room. I stopped a foot away from him and looked up. His face was hidden in the shadows of his cloak, but without a doubt, I knew that he was looking down at me.

"Death," I greeted him.

I jumped when he reached out toward me. My fear was so strong that my entire body started to shake. His arm was covered by his cloak, and his hand was sheathed in a black leather glove. Without a word, he rested his hand on my arm. Instantly, we were transported out of Cain's room and into my own.

He released me, and I instinctively took a step back. I wrapped my arms around my torso to fight off the bitter cold that always accompanied him, not that it did me any good.

"Why me?" I asked suddenly. "Why so much interest in me? I'm nothing."

Instead of speaking, he raised his hands and carefully peeled off one of his gloves. I swallowed roughly when I saw his hand. It looked humanish, but it was far too pale. The skin was almost translucent in its paleness. His fingers were thin, bony even.

"What happens now?" I asked before I could stop myself.

Death was silent for a moment as he took a step toward me. My fear made me want to turn and run, but I knew it was pointless. I was facing *Death*. I couldn't escape him—not now, not ever. He was the one being that every single mortal had to meet.

"Now, I give you my gift, daughter," his voice whispered in my mind.

"What?" I gasped. "Daughter?"

"And there shall be only one, touched by Death, born of Death, who will end the war. Armed with her father's last gift, she will end the war between Heaven and Hell with the Touch of Death." His voice was almost musical, maybe even trancelike.

It lulled me into a peaceful part of myself, a part that didn't even care when he reached out to touch me.

When his fingers wrapped around my wrist, I snapped out of it. I tried to pull my arm free of his grip as a cold so bitter that it was almost unbearable flooded me. No matter how hard I tugged, I couldn't break his grip on my arm. As I desperately struggled against him, the cold intensified until I could no longer bear it. I gasped when my knees suddenly gave out. Instead of falling as I'd expected, Death held me up.

"Do not fear me. You will be stronger than anything they've ever seen. This is the gift I give you."

He was telling me not to fear him? *You're out of your mind,* I thought as my body continued to weaken.

Unable to struggle anymore, I finally stilled and waited for him to rip my soul from my body. The cold intensified until it was the only thing I could think about. My eyes slid shut as every ounce of energy left my body. When I was sure I could take no more, the cold slowly started to change to warmth. It began where Death touched me and spread up my arm and across the rest of my body.

Images of life and death suddenly started flashing behind my eyelids, showing me the story of mankind's rise and fall. In a matter of moments, I watched every soul's death since the beginning of time. It shocked me to see that in each and every single one, Death was not feared but embraced. He was gentle and kind as he took their souls and released them to the angels and demons. I felt the love and affection pouring from the souls and into Death.

Death was not the enemy. He was a friend.

As soon as it'd started, it was over. Death released me, and I slumped to the ground. It took more strength than I would have thought possible to open my eyes and look up at him.

"What have you done to me?" I finally managed to whisper.

"I have given you my one and only gift—the Touch of Death. You and you alone can end this war and bring peace to the souls. You must choose wisely, daughter. Once your decision is made, it cannot be undone."

"Why do you keep calling me daughter?" I asked.

"I will come for you in three days. Your decision must be made by then."

Before I could utter a word, he was gone. The chill followed him, leaving me in a room that suddenly felt sweltering. My eyes slid shut, and I lay there, shaking, trying to remember how to breathe. I felt different, but I wasn't sure why or how.

I swore, I could hear someone calling my name from far away, but I couldn't bring myself to force my eyes back open. Darkness finally settled over me, and thankfully, I passed out.

Twenty-One

When I opened my eyes again, sunlight filtered through my window, lighting up my room. I slowly sat up, testing my body. I felt fine—no, better than fine. I felt excellent. The odd sensations I'd felt the night before were nowhere to be seen. Also, I realized I was no longer on the floor. Someone had put me in my bed.

"Glad to see you're finally awake."

I jerked my head toward the voice.

Cain and Asher sat side by side on the floor, their backs pressed up against my bedroom wall.

"What happened?" I asked.

"We were hoping you could tell us," Cain said.

He and Asher stood. They walked over to my bed and sat down on opposite sides.

"We thought you were dead. Imagine our surprise when the barrier went down, and we rushed over here to find you alive."

"He didn't want to kill me," I said after a moment. "All those times he tried to reach me, he never wanted me dead."

I wasn't sure who my answer surprised more—the brothers or me.

"Then, what did he want?" Asher spoke up for the first time.

"He gave me a gift," I said. It sounded crazy even to my own ears, but I knew it was true.

"What sort of gift?" Cain asked. "Candy and flowers? Maybe he decided to bring you a puppy?"

"The Touch of Death," I said.

Every muscle in Cain's and Asher's bodies instantly tensed up. Apparently, I'd said the magic words. Now, the angel's and demon's feathers were ruffled.

"That's impossible," Asher said. "We lifted you onto your bed. If you possessed the Touch of Death—"

"We'd both be dead right now," Cain finished for him. "Unless it only works once she's truly no longer a part of this realm. That would explain why we can touch her without being blasted into oblivion."

"I don't know what to tell you guys, but I know what he said and what he did. He gave me this gift to end the war you two are fighting in," I told them.

"I don't understand," Asher whispered. "She wasn't supposed to have the gift until after she died. The prophecy—"

"Was never very clear. Come on, Asher. We both know how touchy and vague those things are," Cain said. "Obviously, we're still alive, so the whole anyone-the-soul-with-the-Touch-of- Death-touches-will-die isn't true either. Or maybe it is, and like I said, it only works after she dies."

"I love how you're standing there, calmly discussing my untimely demise," I told Cain, my annoyance evident in my voice.

"Did Death say anything else to you, Ella?" Asher asked, the uncertainty in his voice clear. He seemed to be having a harder time grasping all of this than Cain.

"He told me I had three days to decide which team I'm going to play for." I snorted. "No pressure or anything. I just have to decide if I'm going to destroy the ruler of Heaven or Hell without knowing a thing about them, except for what you two have told me. No offense, but from what I've heard, both Heaven and Hell seem to be full of assholes."

"If you think that, then we've failed," Asher said.

I looked over at him. "What are you talking about?"

"Asher and I weren't sent here to look after you—well, not at first. We were sent because we knew who you were from the beginning. It was our job to convince you to pick one of us over the other," Cain admitted.

"Knew who I was?" I asked.

"The prophecy, remember? We always knew you would be the one to end the battle. Heaven and Hell sent us because...well, we look like a teenage girl's wet dream. Plus, we're the best of the best. Both sides seemed to have the same idea. We had no idea that we would be up against each other until we arrived."

"So, befriending me, spending time with me...it was all a lie to convince me to choose one of you over the other." I looked at Asher. "That's why you kept warning me away from Cain in the beginning. The things you said to me last night…they were just to screw with my head."

"At first, yes, it was just a job to us, but things have changed, Ella. We've both grown attached to you," Asher said. "Things have become far more complicated than anyone thought possible."

"Angels and demons with real feelings. Who would've thought?" I muttered.

Inside, I was hurt even though I shouldn't be. I'd known right from the start that Cain's and Asher's attention wasn't normal. This proved it. Still, I'd grown to care for both of them.

"When the time comes…when I *die*, I have to decide which of you to go with, don't I?" I asked. "It has to be one of you."

Cain nodded. "It does. Whoever you pick will take you to his realm. The other will go home empty-handed."

"And probably end up punished," I added. When neither denied it, I sighed. "I really do hate both realms—or, at least, I hate their leaders."

"Don't," Cain said.

I was surprised that it was him that spoke up instead of Asher.

"Hating both sides will do you no good, Ella. You must pick one," Cain said.

"How?" I demanded. "I know nothing of what is really happening in either." A crazy thought popped into my head. "Wait."

"What?" Asher asked.

"Is there a way you could take me to the realms before I die?" I winced as I mentioned my own death. "That way, I could truly see what I'm up against."

"Are you insane?" Asher demanded.

"No mortal has ever been in a realm before their death, Ella. I'm not sure it's even possible," Cain chimed in.

"It's worth a try, isn't it?" I asked.

"It couldn't hurt," Cain said.

"Seriously?" Asher looked at him. "You're both mental."

Cain shrugged. "What? I say, we each take her to a portal and see if she can pass through. If she can't, no harm done. If she *can*, then she can have a look around to see what she's getting herself into."

"This is insane," Asher muttered. "She can't just waltz right into Heaven and Hell. It's…it's unheard of! And the fact that you're even entertaining this idea of hers, Cain—"

"What's wrong, brother? Are you afraid she'll see something she doesn't like in Heaven?" Cain's tone was arrogant, but the fire in his eyes surprised me.

"Of course not," Asher said after a moment.

"Then, it's settled." I threw my legs over the side of the bed and stood. "Let me get ready, and we'll go."

"What's the hurry?" Cain joked.

I glared at him. "Three days to live, remember?"

"Oh, that." He grinned. "Time moves slower in Heaven and Hell. A day here is like a week there."

"So, you mean to tell me that if this works, I have *weeks* instead of days to live?" I asked.

"Pretty much," Cain answered.

Surprised and even a little bit hopeful over the fact I could live a little longer than anticipated, I hurried over to my closet and pulled out a pair of jeans and a long-sleeved shirt. After grabbing undergarments, I sprinted across the hall to the bathroom and showered quickly. I pulled my still wet hair back into a bun, brushed my teeth, and pulled on my clothes.

Less than five minutes later, I was back in my room, listening to Cain and Asher bicker over whether or not to let me try my plan.

When I couldn't stand to hear any more, I spoke up, "Let's go."

"Go where?" Cain asked. "You haven't told us which realm you want to visit first."

"Take me to Hell." I didn't hesitate with my answer. I knew that going to Hell first was the right decision. Plus, I wouldn't have Asher fighting me every step of the way. "Wow, I never thought I'd say those words."

"If this works, I'll be waiting for you here when you return. Please, be careful," Asher said as he stood and walked over to me. "I can't believe I'm actually going to let you do this."

"Can't you come with me?" I asked.

He shook his head. "Only Cain can enter Hell. When it's time for you to see Heaven, he'll be the one left behind, *if* you can even get in."

"Oh," I said, surprised at how sad it made me to realize I was leaving Asher behind. I leaned forward and tightly wrapped my arms around him. "You be careful, too. If they lay a hand on you, I'll kill them. And when I say it this time, I actually mean it. I *can* kill them." *I just don't know how it works.*

"Be safe, Ella," Asher said as he hugged me back. After a moment, he released me and pulled away.

"You sure about this?" Cain asked as he stood and walked over to me.

"Yes," I said. I wasn't, but I didn't have any other option.

If Death and the brothers were right, then I was the one who would change everything. I needed as much information as I could get even if that meant personally going to Hell and Heaven to get it.

He nodded as he reached out and took my hand in his. Instantly, my room disappeared as he transported us away. I'd managed to catch a final glimpse of Asher. He'd looked sad and maybe even a little bit angry. I hoped that by the time I made it back from Hell, he would forgive me.

I blinked, and when I opened my eyes, we were standing in a forest. Sweltering heat and humidity pressed down around us, almost suffocating me. I pulled my hand away from Cain as I looked around.

"This is Hell?" I watched a group of monkeys up in a tree. "It's not what I was expecting."

Cain laughed. "No, this is the Amazon. I took you to the nearest portal."

"I don't see anything," I said, feeling like a moron.

"Take my hand again," Cain instructed.

I did as he'd said. "Now what?"

"Turn around."

Suddenly nervous, I turned. Before me stood two black doors at least fifty feet tall, and each one had a golden handle shaped like flames.

"Wow," I mumbled.

"You haven't seen anything yet," Cain said as we started walking toward the doors. "Are you ready?"

Every fiber of my being demanded that I turn and run away, but I forced myself to stay where I was. From this moment on, I was no longer the timid and scared little girl who felt cheated because of the things fate had done to her. No, there was no place in my world for that little girl anymore. Fate had laid out a plan for me, a crazy plan, but no matter how scary it got, it was time that I took control. I had to be brave.

"As I'll ever be," I finally said.

Cain reached out and pushed the doors open. "Let's do this."

Then, I walked into Hell.

BOOK TWO COMING SOON! MAKE SURE NOT TO MISS THE RELEASE. JOIN MY MAILING LIST NOW!

http://bit.ly/18Ec6X7

ALSO, CHECK OUT MY WEBSITE FOR MORE INFORMATION ON MY BOOKS AND SALES!

www.authorkarobinson.com

About the Author

K.A. Robinson is the *New York Times* and *USA Today* bestselling author of over fifteen books. She lives in West Virginia with her husband and son. When she isn't writing, she enjoys reading and drinking far too much coffee and Diet Pepsi.

IF YOU ENJOYED ULTIMATE TEMPTATIONS, PLEASE TAKE A MOMENT TO LEAVE A REVIEW. I WOULD REALLY APPRECIATE IT!

Made in the USA
San Bernardino, CA
15 July 2020